THE SPELLBINDING SECRET OF AVERY BUCKLE

Hannah Foley

Kelpies

1

Sprinting out of the school building, Avery Buckle jumped nimbly onto the high brick wall that circled the playground.

"I wish you wouldn't do that," said Low, running to meet her.

Low was Avery's best friend.

"This?" asked Avery, skipping along the top of the wall.

"You're going to fall!" Low called with a gasp, as she leapt gracefully across an open gateway and landed on the other side. "Where have you been? I've been waiting for you."

"Sorry, I got detention." Avery gazed down at him from under her thick black fringe. Her wide eyes were an unusual yellowy green.

"Another one? Let me guess... fidgeting and not sitting still again?"

Avery nodded and made a face. She paused and squinted down the street. Her warm brown skin cooled a shade. From the corner of her eye, she thought she had seen something moving in the shadows. Up on

5

the wall she could see to the far end of the road in both directions, right down to her house at the bottom. It was October and the daylight was fading. Lights blinked on in houses as people returned home from school and work.

As the year had passed into autumn, and the evening shadows had lengthened, Avery had had a growing sense of being followed. It had just been an uneasy feeling to start off with, a prickle down the back of her neck, but it had been mounting and today she was sure that someone, or some*thing*, was lurking in the darkness down the street.

She peered into the dim distance but saw nothing. Taking a deep breath, she tried to slow her racing heart, pushing her hand into her pocket and closing her fingers over the objects nestled there: a rounded piece of sea glass and a small old guidebook with a fold-out map. Immediately her panic eased and a funny glad feeling filled her heart.

"*Pleeease* come down, Avery," pleaded Low nervously. He pushed his glasses back up his gingery freckled nose.

Avery gave the street one last look and sprang onto the pavement below, smoothing her hair with her hands. Her thoughts turned back to her detention. "Don't you ever want to find somewhere you can be yourself, Low? Somewhere you don't have to sit still if that's not who you are?"

"What do you mean?" he asked, hopping about on one foot. "I am myself."

But I'm not, Avery wanted to say.

"Cheer up," called Low, puffing on ahead on his short legs. "It's the Halloween disco tonight."

Avery bounded after him. "Why won't you tell me about your costume?" She had no idea why Low had decided to be so secretive this year.

He shook his head with a smug grin. "You'll have to wait and see!"

"It's not fair, you know what I'm going as."

"That's because it's always the same thing."

Avery stopped outside her front door. Number 58 was no different to any of the other red-brick terraced houses in the street. Frilly net curtains hung at the window and on the sill was a trough of yellow pansies, cheerful in the late afternoon gloom.

Low ran on. "See you there!"

She watched him jog away, his messy tawny hair just visible above his enormous rucksack. It was no doubt full of books, as always. It bumped up and down on his back dangerously, threatening to topple him at any moment.

Avery let herself into the house. The warm scent of baking enveloped her as she dumped her school bag on the hall floor and kicked off her shoes.

"Is that you, sweetie?" Cindy's voice wafted from the kitchen.

"Yes, it's me!" Avery called back with a roll of her eyes. Who else would it be?

"Come through and tell me about your day. I've baked cookies!"

"It's been okay," began Avery, walking into the kitchen. "Detention was kind of annoying—" She stopped mid-sentence.

"Never mind, chick. Look, I've ironed your knickers for you," crooned Cindy, holding up a pair of neatly laundered pants.

"No ironing knickers!" cried Avery. "How many times have we been through this, Cindy? Shirts, yes. Knickers, no!"

Cindy was tall and slender with long delicate hands and dyed golden hair, blow-dried into a fluffy ball. It being Thursday, she was wearing her blue house jacket. She always wore one to protect her clothes when she was cleaning. She had a different colour for each day of the week. Cindy liked everything to be so pristine it gleamed, but that didn't explain why she herself sparkled faintly under the kitchen lights.

Though Cindy tried hard to be like a mother to Avery, nothing could change the fact that she was just a magic spell. A guardian spell conjured to look after her.

Avery sighed.

"Welcome home, sweetheart!" Bob popped his head around the kitchen door, beaming broadly. He had short grey hair and wore spectacles that seemed too small for his round face. Large and jolly, he loved two things: his unusual collection of cheese graters – which he spent a great deal of time polishing – and bad jokes. Like Cindy, Bob shimmered softly under bright light.

"I'm going upstairs to get changed," Avery said quickly, before he could test any of his terrible jokes on her. "It's the school Halloween disco tonight, remember."

"Righto, chick," said Cindy. "Oh, another one of those packages arrived for you. I've X-rayed it, and it's nothing dangerous." Cindy closed her eyes and hummed quietly to herself as she waved her pale hand over a small parcel wrapped up in brown paper and tied with string. She opened her eyes. "Yes, definitely safe. Always worth a second check." She smiled brightly and handed Avery the package.

Avery frowned at Cindy but said nothing. She took the parcel and headed upstairs. Who X-rays every bit of post that comes through the letterbox? A magical pretend parent, that's who.

Once in her bedroom, Avery laid the package on the bed and traced the swirling handwriting with her finger: *Avery Buckle*. It was the sort of writing you found in old books, full of delicate flicks and curls. There was an inky postmark on the parcel in the top right corner that she couldn't quite make out, but no stamp or address. It was very odd. How had it got here?

It had been the same with the mysterious parcels that had brought her the sea glass and the guidebook. There had been no note with them, and no sign of who sent them. The sea glass was frosted white, but looked no different to glass that anyone could pick up on beaches the world over. The edges of the little guidebook curled with age and were mottled with brown specks. It was the sort of thing you might find in a second-hand bookshop. It described a district of Edinburgh called Canonmills. Avery had never been to Scotland and didn't know anyone there, so there was no reason for someone to send her such a thing.

Carefully untying the string on the new parcel, Avery ripped the paper away to reveal a small round object, brown and wrinkled. A peach stone.

Someone had sent her a peach stone.

She pulled the sea glass and the guidebook from her pocket, holding them in one hand and the peach stone in the other. There it was again: that funny glad feeling. She couldn't say why, but when she touched this strange collection of items, she felt her whole body flood with a comforting kind of warmth.

Avery rummaged amongst the torn paper but couldn't find a note. Who was sending her these things? And why?

They'd started to arrive around the same time that Avery had first felt she was being followed. Was that connected, or just a coincidence?

Maybe her real parents had sent them? Avery had never known her mother and father. As far back as she could remember she had lived with Bob and Cindy, two spells conjured up by who knew who to take care of her. Both Bob and Cindy had always been completely honest on that front.

"What exactly *are* you?" Avery had first asked them when she was very small.

The answer was always the same. "We're magic!" Bob would beam. "Our job is to look after something or someone very precious. *We* look after *you*."

"And you have absolutely no idea who conjured you up?" Avery would ask.

"Not a bean!" they would reply. "You've been put here with us to keep you safe, so keep you safe is what we do."

"Safe from what? And are you sure you don't know who my parents are?" Avery would persist.

"Not a clue on either count, I'm afraid." Bob would shake his head, but Cindy would look at Avery sadly.

"*Were*, we don't know who your parents *were*, Avery. You're the last of the Cat Fae, and if you're the last, it stands to reason there can't be any others."

"But you don't *know* that, do you?" Avery would say stubbornly. "And what exactly is a Cat Fae anyway?"

"Oh well, that's easy," Bob would nod. "A Cat Fae is you. Part-human and part-cat – but entirely special."

And that was the nub of it, because being brought up by two spells wasn't the only unusual thing about Avery Buckle.

Avery had a tail, a long black furry tail, which she kept carefully hidden away.

2

Her tail was the reason Avery always went to the school Halloween disco dressed as a cat. Halloween was the only time in the whole year when she could show her tail and no one would bat an eyelid. If you had asked her, she would have said it was just part of her, in the same way that Low wore glasses or some of the kids in her class spoke different languages. She would have said it was a 'normal difference'.

But deep down Avery knew nobody else had a tail, and although it was great for helping her balance and climb where no one else could, it did make sitting neatly in class very tricky. And because no one else had one, Avery kept her tail hidden under her clothes, except on Halloween.

Putting the finishing touches to her costume, Avery tucked the peach stone into her pocket along with the other objects. She had one hand on the front door when Bob appeared in the hall, pulling on his coat.

"I'll walk you round, sweetheart," he said.

"Honestly, I'm fine, Bob. It's just at the end of the street." Avery had been hoping to walk to school on her own. It wasn't that she didn't love Bob and Cindy, but she preferred to limit their interactions with other adults. She'd been in too many awkward situations where they'd cheerily got things very wrong without realising. Like the time Bob had congratulated one of the mums at the school gate on how 'wonderfully round' she was. Or when Cindy loudly boycotted the cake stall at the school summer fete for selling fairy cakes, accusing them of cruelty to mythical creatures and explaining that their fur alone showed how unsuitable faeries were for putting into cakes.

"You'll miss *What's in the Box?*" Avery said, hoping the thought of Bob's favourite TV show would stall him.

"No, no," he replied, peering up and down the street into the gathering dusk, a small frown flitting across his face. "It's getting dark, and you never know who's about." He held the front door open for Avery.

She hadn't told Bob or Cindy about the feeling of being followed, but Bob's nervous frown made her wonder if he somehow already knew. She decided she would ask him about it later – if she brought it up now he might not let her go to the disco at all.

"What's a cat's favourite colour?" Bob asked as he closed the front door behind them and they made their way along the street.

"Purr-ple," sighed Avery.

"Why did the horse cross the road?" he continued cheerily.

"Because someone shouted 'hey!'" Avery dutifully replied.

In spite of the fact she'd heard them all before, Bob's terrible jokes slowly started to make Avery smile, and by the time they were in sight of the school she was actually laughing.

"Would you mind dropping me here?" she asked, hoping Bob wouldn't be offended.

"Ho, ho," he chuckled. "Too cool for old Bob, eh? Alright then. I'll just watch you in."

"Thanks, Bob." Avery gave him a squeeze and darted off. As she reached the school steps she turned and gave him a little wave. He waved back, and she could hear him whistling the *What's in the Box?* theme tune as he turned for home.

Inside the disco, Avery swept across the floor, an ink-black silhouette against the dancing lights of red and gold and green. Witches and monsters, ghosts and devils wheeled around her. Avery's tail flew out behind her, seeming to curl gently this way and that of its own accord. She felt a thrill of freedom. Tonight, for once, she could just be herself.

Low ran up to her, all feathers and beak, dressed as an owl. "So, what do you think?" he asked, arms held out so she could fully admire his costume mastery.

"Brilliant!" she grinned. "It suits you."

He grinned back. "Have you tried these wriggly worms? I don't think we had them last year." He offered her a crumpled paper bag full of warm, sticky worm-shaped sweets.

She grimaced. "I think I'll pass, thanks."

Low shrugged. "Don't you get bored of always coming as a cat?" he asked between enthusiastic chews. "Your tail's always cool, though - will you let me try it on?" Before Avery could stop him, he'd given it a hard pull.

"OW!" Avery yelped, glaring at him.

"Avery!" Low stared back, mouth open, a half-chewed gummy worm in danger of escaping. "Your tail, it's... it's a-attached. And it's warm... like it's... r-real!"

But Avery didn't get the chance to reply. Suddenly, there was a high-pitched screeching sound and the music came to an abrupt halt.

The disco lights flickered and then went out, plunging the school hall into thick darkness. Then there was full-scale panic; children screamed, and bodies bumped and bounced off each other in the chaos.

Avery froze.

Something didn't feel right. Something was far more not-right than a simple blackout at the school disco.

She had the creeping, uneasy feeling again; she could sense a dark, menacing presence.

Avery looked around the hall with dread. Her night

vision (a handy benefit of being part cat) helped her to see movement through the pitch-black. She stared in horror as a dense shape began to grow out of the floor. Within it was a writhing, thrashing mass of shadowy creatures.

Avery's heart pounded.

"There *was* someone watching in the shadows!" she whispered to herself in horror. "I didn't imagine it. And now they're here, and they're after me!"

The thought hit her like a speeding train. She didn't know how she knew this with so much certainty, she just did, deep down in her heart. She knew they were bad, and she had to get away. But where was Low?

Avery could feel the shadows slithering and snarling, hissing doom and destruction into the air. Above the shifting shapes she could make out teachers directing children to safety, but they couldn't see the creatures in the darkness – the creatures that were coming for Avery.

She had to get out.

Swiftly and silently she dodged through the crowds, deftly winding her way until she found the exit. But out in the foyer more writhing shadows blocked her path, snatching out for her with long twisting arms. They had no real faces, no eyes or noses, but Avery could see rows of small sharp teeth in gaping mouths and black, flicking tongues. She backed away, groping with her hands against the wall, until she reached out into empty space.

The door to the kitchens.

She dived inside, knocking a stack of pans off a work surface with a clatter. The lights were out in here too, but Avery could make out her surroundings enough to be sure there was no way out.

Panic filled her, and she unconsciously put her hand in her pocket, wrapping her fingers around her collection of objects. She closed her eyes and felt her heart steady, her mind clear. Wasn't there supposed to be some way up into the school attic from the kitchens?

She began opening doors, finding only cupboards, then, with a flood of relief, discovering a steep staircase behind a latched door. Avery leapt up the steps and heaved the cover of a wooden hatch out of the way, then pulled herself through and crouched on the edge of the hole.

The attic smelt musty, and it was littered with broken chairs. A square of moonlight at the furthest end illuminated the slanting space.

A window!

Heart pounding, she sprinted for it, not daring to look behind her. She imagined the shadowy figures filling the kitchens below her like smoke.

Bright stars pricked the night sky outside, but no matter how hard she pushed, the window wouldn't budge.

"No, no, no!" Avery muttered desperately, feeling the nails holding the edges of the frame shut.

Suddenly, the fur on her tail stood up on end. She didn't need to turn around to know that the shadows had found her. She was out of time.

Picking up a broken chair leg, she shielded her face as she swung it back and blindly began smashing at the glass. The cold night air rushed in just as she felt hot breath on her neck.

As a clawed tendril of dense shadow snaked towards her leg, Avery scrambled through the smashed window and jumped.

She leapt into the night sky, an arched silhouette against the white full moon. Momentarily she dropped, twisting in mid-air, then her legs swung up in front of her. Avery felt a sickening tightening of her costume as she lurched to a halt and was pulled upwards. She hung dejectedly, too weary to struggle. They'd got her.

"Did we get away?" a familiar voice panted from above.

Avery wriggled around in alarm, briefly in freefall again as strong talons lost their grip before gently regaining their hold.

"Woah, you're heavier than you look."

"Low? Is that you? You're… an owl! A real one! And you're flying!"

"Yeah, though not for much longer if I have to keep carrying you."

"Right, right," said Avery, suspending disbelief for the sake of urgency. Peering round, she scanned the roof of the school hall but there was nothing there. The shadows had gone.

"I'm actually not joking," wheezed Low. "You're really heavy."

"Don't worry, I've got a weird feeling something'll come to me," replied Avery, feeling almost giddy with relief.

"Something'll come to you? That's your plan? You've just been attacked by some kind of terrifying shadow-monster-thingys and I'm straining every feather to rescue you and that's your—"

Zing, zip, zing, bop!

Low was cut-off mid-sentence.

A small, brown, round something had just flown up out of Avery's pocket, knocking Low off course. They both cried out in panic. For the third time that night Avery found herself in freefall, clutching at her best friend with one hand, the other frantically fumbling to catch the flying object.

"The peach stone!" she exclaimed, plucking it out of the air. It was zinging away like a hoverfly in a hay meadow. "Hang on, Low!"

Clinging to the stone for dear life, the pair were pulled across the night sky at rapid speed. Although they didn't yet know it, they were heading north.

3

Avery's teeth soon started to chatter as she whizzed through the cold night air. Her thin cat costume flapped and flicked in the icy wind. She briefly wondered if there was any part of her body that wasn't covered with goose bumps, but the thought didn't trouble her for long. It was pushed out by other more important questions racing around her mind, like: what *were* those shadowy things? And since when did peach stones start flying? Come to that, when did her *best friend* start flying? She adjusted her grip on Low, whose teeth sounded as if they were chattering more than Avery's.

He had looked just like an enormous owl back there, entirely covered in tawny feathers. But his shape was changing now. The soft down was slowly disappearing, and the powerful talons that had caught her were lengthening into normal legs and feet again. He was turning back into a boy.

The moon shone down from above as, far below,

the lights of cities and towns flashed past in neon clusters through the gaps in the clouds. They were travelling incredibly fast. Avery had no idea how long they had been airborne, but she was soaked to the skin and her arm was painfully stiff from desperately hanging onto the peach stone.

With a sudden dip, they began to lose height, breaking through the plump clouds until they finally started to slow, flying over a city crammed between the wide flow of glinting water in one direction and dark hills in the other. She could see higgledy-piggledy rooftops jostling for space either side of a long, straight street heading to an old castle.

Without warning, the peach stone swerved sharply and Avery found herself plummeting down towards busy traffic. Lamp posts stood in puddles of orange light on wet pavements, and a column of car headlights waited at a crossing. The peach stone came to an abrupt halt in front of an imposing stone building, hovering a couple of metres off the ground.

"C-could you not take us all the way d-down?" Avery asked the peach stone through chattering teeth, her feet swinging in the air. "Er, p-please?"

It jiggled as if irritated by Avery's question.

"For g-goodness' sake!" she said, looking up.

The peach stone had stopped at the level of some big white letters over the building's enormous front door.

"Oh, h-hang on. I s-see. The N-National Library of S-Scotland," Avery read aloud. With that, the peach stone dropped to the pavement and rolled into the gutter, depositing Avery and Low in a tangled heap on the damp doorstep.

"W-what's going on?" stuttered Low, disoriented from the rapid travel.

Avery dashed to grab the stone before rainwater carried it down a nearby drain. "Are you alright, Low? I think we're supposed to go in here." She looked up at the forbidding door.

Low gaped. "Where are we?"

"We're in Scotland. Edinburgh, I think." There had been a picture of the castle in her old guidebook. "This peach stone brought us here." She held it up in the dim lamplight.

"This is ridiculous!" Low snorted. "Peach stones don't fly."

"Neither do people," Avery retorted. "You never told me you could fly… or that you had feathers!"

Low raised an eyebrow. "Says the girl who's been hiding the fact that she has a tail! And what were those shadowy things back at the disco?" he asked, scrambling to his feet.

Avery didn't know, so how could she answer? She felt incredibly weary: cold, wet and thoroughly confused. All she wanted was for Cindy to come along with some dry clothes and give her a big hug.

If truth be told, she didn't know why she hadn't told Low about being Cat Fae. She knew he'd like her just the same. Maybe keeping it a secret had become too much of a habit. She turned to him and shrugged. "It's not the easiest thing to fit into conversation, you know. Oh yeah Low, by the way, I'm part cat."

Low frowned and looked at the ground.

"Anyway, what are *you?*" she asked, suddenly feeling cross. He'd kept secrets too.

He sighed and shook his head. "I have no idea. I kind of... keep turning into an owl. I'm getting better at controlling it, but it's a really new thing, like only in the last year. And to be honest, it's totally freaking me out."

They stood in silence for a few minutes, neither of them knowing what to say.

"Come on, let's just deal with one thing at a time, shall we?" Avery gave him a placatory smile as she popped the peach stone into her pocket. "Like finding out why we've been brought here." She looked up at the imposing stone façade and wooden double doors of the library. "It doesn't look very open. Maybe this'll do it..." She lifted the heavy metal doorknocker with both hands, letting it drop with an ominous clang.

There was silence, then a scrabbling sound came from behind the door and a shutter on a small glassless window shot open. Something with eight bulbous black eyes peered through at them.

Low jumped. "What is *that?*"

"Library's closed," said a husky voice. The shutter shot back into place, only to open again seconds later. "Sorry, Miss Buckle. Mab's orders. I'm only allowed to let in those who are expected… and you aren't."

"Do you know this… person?" hissed Low, not taking his eyes from the window.

"No!" Avery hissed back. "I think I might remember meeting someone like *that.*"

"Then how do they know your name?" persisted Low.

"I have no idea!"

As one, the multitude of eyes flicked over to Low and blinked. "Who's that?"

"This is Low," explained Avery. "Look, I think we're supposed to come in here. This brought us." She held up the peach stone.

From somewhere behind the door a silky voice called out, "Edgar dear, who's there?"

The eyes blinked with alarm and a giant hairy hand covered the window, muffling the conversation. "It's Avery, Miss Cassandra, but I've orders not to let anyone in who's not expected."

"Avery?" The silky voice sounded surprised. "Orders won't mean Avery."

There was a pause, then the shutter closed again and they heard the jangle of keys and the sound of many bolts being undone. The heavy door creaked opened, casting a warm glow onto the wet pavement. Avery and Low cautiously stepped inside.

The creature known as Edgar scrambled to shut the door behind them, his long hairy arms working the locks and bolts quickly back into place. While his arms were each at least two metres long, his two legs were short and squat. He held up a badly fitting pair of purple corduroy trousers with one hand as he stood on tiptoes to peek back out of the small window into the deserted street. His face was small and round, entirely taken up by all those eyes, surrounded by tufts of grey whiskers.

Low counted Edgar's limbs on his fingers. "One, two, three, four, five, six, seven, *eight*. Avery, I think he's a spider!" he whispered.

"An enormous one," she nodded, equally mystified.

"And he's wearing clothes!" Low whispered again.

Avery made silent shushing signals at Low as Edgar turned around.

"All quiet," he harrumphed, slumping back against the door with relief.

"Avery, welcome!" The most beautiful woman Avery had ever seen smiled down at her. She wore a long satin dress with a high neck and cones of lace at the cuffs, flame-red hair tumbling over her shoulders. She seemed so pleased to see them that Avery instantly felt herself relax.

Edgar loitered at her elbow clutching at his waistcoat and wringing his many hands. "But Miss Cassandra, what will Mab say?"

"Don't worry, Edgar," the woman said sweetly. "I'll explain."

Avery and Low trotted to keep up with the woman as she led them away from Edgar and the foyer. They peered around curiously at the silent library as they followed.

"I can see you don't recognise me, Avery," said the woman, smiling back at them.

"No, I'm sorry," Avery replied. "Have we met?"

"I'm Cassandra. I made a promise to look after you when you were a baby. Myself and the others of course. How are Bob and Cindy?"

"They're well... Wait, how do you know Bob and Cindy? Did you conjure them?"

Cassandra laughed as she guided them towards a grand staircase. It was a wonderful tinkly laugh, and Avery thought she'd never heard such a nice sound before. "Ah you've rumbled them, have you? Ceridwen will be disappointed. I think they were her creation."

"What do you mean 'creation'?" asked Low, brow furrowed.

"They're magic," explained Avery.

27

"Magic?" spluttered Low.

Avery shrugged.

"Right. More secrets," he sighed. "Though that explains why Cindy's baking always tastes so good."

Cassandra laughed again, pushing open a pair of double doors and gliding into an enormous dimly lit room stacked row-upon-row full of bookshelves.

"This is where the bulk of the library's collection is, but there's lots more archived in vaults beneath the building too," she explained, ushering them on towards a flickering light coming from a tall, wide cupboard set in the furthest wall. The doors of the cupboard were propped open by tottering piles of books.

"So many books..." Low said in wonder, staring around the library with his mouth open. He reached out to grab one but Avery batted his hand away. She knew from experience that if she let Low loose in a library they might not find him for days.

"Oh yes, and there are some wonderful maps," said Cassandra. "For the last three hundred years they've been collecting every book ever published." She paused. "It's so nice to be back in Edinburgh. I was born here, you know, and my father had land here, but that was a long time ago—"

Cassandra was cut off by a loud voice roaring across the silent library: "AVERRRY!"

This was followed by the pounding of feet so huge that the floor bounced with each step.

"Rolling cauldrons!" cried Cassandra. "It's Glaurt. Take cover!"

Glaurt was a troll, and was as wide and as tall as the front end of a double-decker bus. As he approached at speed, his tiny eyes were focused only on Avery and his thick arms were spread wide in joyful anticipation.

"Slow down!" yelled Avery, waving her hands in front of her, but the troll had built up too much momentum. As he tried to slow, he stepped on a nearby book trolley, which acted like an awkward roller skate, careering towards them carrying Glaurt's colossal bulk.

"Run!" shouted Cassandra.

If the trolley brake hadn't stuck fast at just that moment, they would almost certainly have been flattened. As it was, Glaurt flew through the air, slid along the shiny library floor on his large belly, and came to a stop only millimetres from their fleeing heels.

"Glaurt, you must be more careful!" scolded Cassandra. "What have we told you about running indoors?"

"AVERY!" was all Glaurt could say as he jumped up and hugged her, happily swinging her from side to side.

Avery found herself squeezed against the troll's rock-like chest. He smelled like over-ripe bananas and old socks.

Low tapped one of Glaurt's enormous ankles. "Er, Mister Glaurt, sir, could you put her down now, please? I don't think she can breathe."

Glaurt paid no attention, hoisting Avery onto his shoulder and marching off towards an open cupboard, crooning, "Glaurt so happy to see Avery!"

"Come along, we'd better follow them." Cassandra picked up her skirts and took Low's hand as they hurried after the retreating troll.

4

"Glaurt! What is the meaning of all this noise?" a sharp voice called out from the cupboard.

It was a large cupboard, but Glaurt was an even larger troll. When he stooped to enter, his hairless head went through with no trouble but his shoulders wedged fast. He wiggled and squirmed, before finally giving a muffled roar of annoyance.

Cassandra raised her eyes to the ceiling. "Come on, he'll need a push," she said to Low, rolling up her elegant sleeves.

Glaurt jerked and jiggled while Cassandra and Low shoved at his enormous bottom.

"Heave!" commanded Cassandra through gritted teeth.

Glaurt burst through the door with a pop, marching off into the interior, Avery now helplessly carried under one arm.

Low peered after them. Dark shelves lined the cupboard walls on both sides, stacked neatly with piles of paper, pens and notebooks. A plume of pages had fluttered to the floor in Glaurt's wake. Right at the furthest end, Low could see light coming from an open door. An open door in the back of a cupboard?

"In you go," said Cassandra.

Low frowned at her. "But it's a stationery cupboard."

"Indeed."

"And there's door in the back of it."

She smiled. "Yes."

Low stopped in front of the cupboard entrance and shook his head. "I don't like cupboards. I got shut in the laundry cupboard by accident once when I little. It took me an hour to get out."

Cassandra nodded. "Yes, laundry cupboards can be like that. Temperamental. Stationery cupboards are an altogether different thing."

Low didn't look convinced.

"Have you never felt a tingle when you opened a brand-new notebook?" she asked. "All those crisp, fresh pages full of possibility. Or the thrill of the first mark made by a pen no one has ever used before?"

"I remember it was quite exciting when I got my handwriting badge at school," conceded Low. "But I don't see what that's got to do with it."

"Pens. Paper. These things are full of magic; down the spine, inside the nib – full to the brim with some of the strongest magic around. So can you imagine what happens when you have piles of fresh new notebooks, pens and paper all together in one place?" Cassandra leaned into the cupboard, closed her eyes and inhaled deeply. "Magic."

"Magic?" repeated Low.

"Can't you smell it? It's wonderful. And right at the back, very little air gets in. There the magic collects, making it the perfect spot for a door – a portal if you will."

Low looked worried. "To where?"

Cassandra smiled enigmatically.

Low peered into the cupboard again. He could see a room on the other side of the open door that didn't match the library at all. "That room through there isn't part of the library, is it?" said Low.

Cassandra gestured for him to enter. "It is today. Now come along, Mab hates to be kept waiting."

Low moved into the cupboard and stared at the open door. Planks of wood had been roughly nailed around it, as if someone had made the hole too big and had to patch it up afterwards. The door itself looked like the front door to a house, painted a deep mossy green with a tarnished brass handle. Above it a flickering lantern swung on a claw-shaped hook.

Low stepped through and found himself in a cramped

entryway. Heaped up on either side was an enormous selection of footwear, from old men's slippers to knee-high, lace-up boots, and bright-green wellingtons with frog faces on the toes. Long black cloaks hung from hooks on the walls, and above them were high shelves stuffed full of hats of every description.

He moved beyond the entryway into a lit room. It smelt of leather, and had soft, warm walls, dark brown in colour and curved to a high point above. Down the centre of the room was a long mahogany table, surrounded by seven ornately carved chairs with frayed cushions. The table was stacked high with books and papers, and above it a cloud of small balls of light whizzed and whirred.

"Do I have to keep repeating myself?" came the sharp voice again. "Glaurt! What is the meaning of all this noise?"

Glaurt stood in front of a stern-faced woman with the same flame-red hair as Cassandra. He placed Avery down, patting her gently towards the woman. "Avery's here!" the troll beamed.

The woman looked shocked, if not faintly appalled, but quickly recovered.

"Avery, you are most welcome." She raised her arms regally. "As you can see, we are currently availing ourselves of the National Library here in Edinburgh."

"I'm sorry," Avery said, thoroughly confused and slightly queasy after her trip by troll. "This is a lot to take in…"

Cassandra smiled again and pointed out through the door. "It's magic, Avery. Out there is the National Library of Scotland in Edinburgh, and in here is the study at Cunningfoot End."

"Study? Cunningfoot End? You make it sound like there's a whole house back here," said Avery, noticing openings to dark, rounded passageways at the far end of the room.

"Indeed, a witches' house," interrupted the sharp-voiced woman, inspecting both Avery and Low through a glass monocle on a gold chain. "The magical world exists in the in-between spaces. Have you ever thought you've seen something out of the corner of your eye, and as soon as you look, whatever you thought was there is gone? Well, that is where the magical realm is. Between the cracks in the pavement, on the tip of your tongue, down the back of the sofa, just out of sight, in the gaps between the floorboards, *and* in the stationery cupboard at the National Library of Scotland."

She peered at Avery. "I take from this that you don't remember much of Cunningfoot, or in fact, of us?"

"No," Avery replied. "I'm sorry… I don't know you, any of you at all. But you seem to know me."

Avery's head was spinning. Magical cupboards, trolls and witches — how could they possibly know her while she couldn't remember any of them? She was certain she'd never met them before, or visited this place, unless it had been when she was a baby.

"I am Mab, one of the seven witches of Cunningfoot End," the woman pronounced. "We are an alliance of witches from around the globe, come to the library to look for something extremely important..." For a moment Mab paused and looked helplessly around her, as if she had lost her train of thought. "Yes, something very important. Something that... escapes me just at this moment."

She shook herself and continued. "You have met Edgar, Cunningfoot's porter. And Glaurt..." Mab pursed her lips. The troll puffed his chest out. "Well, Glaurt is the caretaker for want of a better term. He has a... talent for establishing new entry points." Mab waved in the direction of the entrance and Low thought of the nailed planks on the back of the cupboard.

"I make the holes!" Glaurt said proudly.

"Indeed." Mab gave a sniff. The troll's method obviously lacked some of her preferred finesse. "You have met Cassandra."

Cassandra nodded and smiled encouragingly at Avery.

"That is Kikimora," said Mab.

A sharp-featured, olive-skinned woman wearing

a neatly pinned headscarf waved from between two precariously balanced towers of books.

"Over there is Ceridwen."

Mab signalled a large jolly woman in a red-and-white polka-dot dress at the far end of the table. Her rosy cheeks danced as she called out, "Hello, my lovelies!"

"This is Lilith."

A small dark-haired woman with a heavy fringe and a tawny-brown complexion blinked rapidly at Avery through an enormous pair of round spectacles.

"Jezebel has gone to put the kettle on, and Baba is somewhere around. We reside here at Cunningfoot End, but obviously," Mab paused again, "the doors of Cunningfoot may open anywhere: the linen cupboard at the Ritz Hotel in Paris, in the ladies' toilets of the New York Police Department HQ, even in the tiger enclosure at London Zoo. There are doors all over the place, if you know where to look. So there we are, introductions done." Mab came close to Avery, eyeing her again through the monocle. "But what I want to know is – what exactly *you* are doing here?"

Everything about Mab was stern and severe, all the way from her tightly buttoned-up dress and icy stare, right down to her pointed black boots. Avery suddenly felt nervous. "Well, we-we-we…"

"'We?'" repeated Mab. "Who is this 'we'?"

Flustered, Avery turned to look for Low. He came scampering forward, cheeks burning.

"Low Hoskings," he said, stretching out a trembling hand. Mab took it coldly, but as skin touched skin, she jumped. She grabbed Low's hand and pulled him towards her, scrutinising him ferociously.

The other witches darted over.

"What is it, Mab?" they asked. "What have you seen?"

"He's an owl!" squawked Kikimora, sniffing Low's armpit.

"Not all the time," exclaimed Low, shrinking in on himself under the witches' interested gaze. "Mostly I'm boy."

"A Hoolet!" cried Mab, eyes ablaze. "Your species is extinct, boy!"

"A what? And what do you mean, my *species*?" repeated Low.

"Ooo arrr your parentssss? Arrr zey owelsss?" asked Lilith, as she inspected Low's fingernails and spun him on the spot.

"I'm sorry?" he asked.

"She said, who are your parents? Are they owls?" Kikimora repeated slowly and loudly as if he were very stupid.

"N-n-no," replied Low. "They're just normal humans and they really are my parents. I checked when

I first started… well… y'know…" He flapped his arms awkwardly. "Being owly."

"Won't they miss you, love?" asked Ceridwen fussing with his hair.

"Probably not," replied Low, ducking out of the witch's reach. "They hardly notice me when I'm there. I've been roosting in the attic for weeks and they haven't batted an eyelid. They're always working."

"But do they *look* a bit owly?" persisted Kikimora.

Low shrugged. "Well, I suppose they do a bit. When they're in their wigs and gowns especially. They're both court judges."

"Not purr-aaps fullee owel zen," mused Lilith. "But a remnant uv Hoolet blud zat 'as come togezer in zis boy."

"Gordon at the Owl Centre would know for definite," added Kikimora.

"Well I never," said Ceridwen, fisting her large hands on her even larger hips. "What do you make of that, Mab?"

"Interesting!" replied Mab fiercely, beginning to pace the floor. "Avery, you still haven't answered my questions."

"We were attacked. Low saved my life. We only just got away!" Avery blurted out, feeling small, lost and very confused.

Mab stopped pacing instantly. "Quickly, girl, by whom, where and when? I need details."

"At the school Halloween disco. They were all shadowy, the things that attacked us. They sort of came out of the ground in a big black mass, and they had these long grabby claws. They were snarling and hissing, and they didn't have any faces but they had teeth. They were horrible. I only saw them properly tonight, but I've felt for a while now that there was someone in the dark... watching me." Avery's eyes brimmed with tears and Cassandra put a gentle arm around her. "Then this evening they were everywhere. If it hadn't been for Low, they would have got me. What are they? What do they want with me?"

There was a potent silence before Mab replied, "The Badoch... They're shapeless beings that can merge together to make themselves more powerful when they're on the hunt. They come from the Mamores mountain range, north of Kinlochleven. They're creatures of shadow, nasty things. You had a lucky escape."

Avery felt a chill run down her spine remembering the feel of warm breath on her neck before she'd leapt from the attic window.

Mab drummed her fingertips on her bottom lip in thought. "How could they have moved so far south? And why?" She glared at Avery. "But more to the point, how did *you* get here?"

Avery held up the peach stone. "This flew up out of my pocket and brought us here. It came in the post. I've been getting strange parcels." Avery broke into a broad smile. "And Cassandra says you all promised to look after me – so it must have been you, mustn't it?"

There was an awkward silence.

"…Mustn't it?"

Mab glared accusingly at the other witches, who all avoided her gaze, busily examining their fingernails or suddenly finding something on the floor very fascinating.

"Yes, it must have been," replied Mab through gritted teeth. "Let me see that," she demanded, holding out a pale spidery hand.

Avery dropped the stone into Mab's palm. The instant the stone touched her skin, there was a loud sizzle. Mab yelped and dropped it, clutching her burnt hand to her chest.

"Now then!" exclaimed Ceridwen.

From some dark corner of the room there was a rhythmic flapping of feet and a small figure dressed in what looked like hundreds of cardigans scurried in amongst them. Her russet-brown skin was creased with laughter lines and a cloud of white hair stood in a halo around her face. On her feet she wore an enormous pair of old man's slippers that made a loud slapping noise on the floor when she walked.

Taking Mab's hand, she tutted over the burn mark before stroking it with a stubby finger, from which there came a spark of bright light. The skin of Mab's hand crinkled for a second before healing completely.

"Did you see that?" Low exclaimed to no one in particular.

"Yes, Baba's good like that," replied Kikimora matter-of-factly.

Baba pulled a large white handkerchief out of her pocket and used it to pick the peach stone up from the floor, eyeing Avery thoughtfully.

"I'll be keeping this if you don't mind, my dear," she said, her brown eyes twinkling.

There was a clatter of tea things as a woman with bronzed skin and bright blue hair piled high on top of her head arrived, an overloaded tea tray floating along behind her.

"Oh, don't tell me!" she exclaimed in a Texan drawl. "I've missed all the action."

Just then, a loud banging thundered through the library:

BOOM! BOOM! BOOM!

It echoed down the corridors and through the open door of the stationery cupboard, quickly followed by the sound of Edgar shouting.

"No, Jezebel," said Kikimora cheerfully. "It sounds like you've arrived just in time."

5

"Glaurt, go and see what the fuss is about!" instructed Mab, who had quickly recovered her poise.

The troll threw a disappointed glance at the tea tray and stomped back through the entry way, and out of the front door, knocking down some of the hanging wood from the back of the cupboard as he went.

"Now then," said Ceridwen. "Shall I pour?"

But as the teacups were passed around it became harder and harder to ignore the thudding and shouting, which seemed to be getting louder and nearer. Mab tutted as a particularly big thud caused her to spill half her tea into her saucer. There was a sudden ominous silence before a dark-haired boy, just a bit older than Avery and Low, strode into the room. He pushed his leather cape behind him as he sat down heavily, plonking his muddy boots up on the table. Mab looked like she'd swallowed a golf ball. He glared at her. "Surprised to see me, Mab?"

Jezebel handed the boy a cup of tea. "Ghilli, honey, you're just in time. Two sugars, right?"

Ghilli shot Mab another hard glare as he took the tea. "Jezebel, you're an angel." Leaning back on his chair, he raised his teacup and pronounced, "Your good health, ladies."

Kikimora giggled and Lilith raised her eyebrows behind her teacup.

Mab was not impressed.

"Feet off my table, young man," she commanded, sending a purple spark from one finger that bumped his feet back to the floor with a puff of smoke. Ghilli jumped up, his cheeks ablaze under his chestnut-brown skin.

"Oh, so you're not ignoring me now, Mab?" he asked, angry again. "You know why I'm here. There's trouble at Inchmahome and since you don't seem to be in any rush to help, the Elders sent me to pay a visit."

"Sit down a minute, Ghilli, honey and tell us all about it," replied Jezebel soothingly.

"And while you're there could you tell us what you've done with Edgar and Glaurt?" added Ceridwen, arms folded.

Ghilli sat back down, slamming his boots back on the table and glaring at Mab. "They're tied up in the library's cloakroom," he said rebelliously. "They wouldn't let me in and I'd come all this way."

"I'll just go and untie them, I will," tutted Ceridwen, hurrying off.

"Now," said Jezebel. "What's happening at Inchmahome?"

"What's happening?" Ghilli nearly choked on his tea and glared again at Mab. "She knows all about it. Get *her* to tell you."

"If you wouldn't mind, Ghilli, I think we'd all like to hear about it from you," said Jezebel, patting his shoulder.

"In the dead of night the Badoch have been creeping over the hills and attacking faeries, picking them off one by one. By the time the alarm's raised they've vanished into the night again." He took an angry gulp of tea. "On my way here I received news of another assault. The victim was brought to Inchmahome barely alive this very evening. And do you know what the Badoch have been doing to them?" Ghilli turned to the assembled group. "Cutting the faeries' tails off!"

He held up his own tail. Avery's eyes widened. She'd never seen someone else with a tail before. Ghilli's was much longer than hers, and wiry like a leopard's, covered in thick black fur with white spots. Low elbowed her, whispering not-at-all quietly, "He's got a tail!"

Ghilli glanced up at the sound of Low's voice, noting them both with confused recognition, but turned back to the witches, who had erupted with cries of disbelief.

"What?"

"The Badoch attacking faeries!"

"But that's not all," continued Ghilli grimly. "An ollipheist has been harassing Inchmahome's borders."

"An ollipheist? A bewitched dragon!" cried Cassandra, clutching her neck. "It can't be true."

"But it is," declared Ghilli. "And *she* knew all about it."

Every eye in the room turned to Mab. She looked like she would gladly have squashed Ghilli under her boot.

"Is zis true, Mab?" asked Lilith blinking.

"Yes," she replied. "But only since this morning—"

"Liar!" shouted Ghilli. "We sent word more than a week ago."

"The message was waylaid, boy!" hissed Mab. "What arrived here was half-dead and badly damaged. I could barely decipher it. Don't believe me?"

Mab reached high up her sleeve with her opposite hand and pulled out a metal tin. Laying it on the table, she opened the lid and lifted something out. Avery stood on tiptoes to see. The remains of a beetle about the size of a side plate lay on Mab's hand. Its carapace was scorched with black burn marks, but it was still possible to see that it had been a beautiful blue metallic colour. One limp wing hung from its side.

"I do declare, that is the work of a bewitched dragon if ever I saw it," declared Jezebel stoutly.

Mab lifted the burnt carapace up, revealing a small cavity underneath, and with her little finger she edged out a charred piece of parchment. It was all that remained of Ghilli's message.

"You see." She looked pointedly at Ghilli. "It was fortunate you chose to send a shield beetle. A herald bug would never have made it here."

Ghilli was staring hard at the messenger beetle, his chin set firm. Avery could see he was shocked but trying to hide it.

"The tragedy that has befallen your people is terrible," said Mab, carefully placing the burnt remains back in the tin. "But it is only one piece of a much greater terror. Did you know that Peat Hags have been seen in daylight hours in the Cairngorms? We have received news that Finn-folk have been carrying out brazen raids on the Western Isles. There has even been a report of a flock of Sluagh circling Suilven. Something is brewing that has the power to disrupt not just the magical world, but the human world too. And where are the great wizarding clans of Scotland whose business it is to maintain balance in this land?" Mab threw her hands up into the air. "Vanished or burying their heads in the sand. What do you think we are doing in this library? Having a nice holiday, perhaps? No, we're looking for answers! But as usual Ghilli Dhu thinks he knows everything."

"Well, what have you found out then?" demanded the faery.

Mab looked taken aback. "We... we... umm, well. One moment, it will come to me..."

Avery and Low had been largely forgotten with the abrupt entrance of Ghilli. They had watched the goings-on open-mouthed, casting questioning glances at each other. But now Baba was gently pulling at their sleeves, drawing them away from the brightly lit table towards one of the dark earthen passages that led off the study.

"That's quite enough excitement for one night. I'm sure you're hungry, aren't you?" she asked. She beckoned one of the balls of whirring light from above the table to follow them, and Avery and Low stumbled after her, suddenly aware of their tiredness.

"Would there be any chance of some warm milk?" asked Avery as they made their way through the passageways. The place was like a rabbit warren, full of twisting tunnels and shadowy nooks and crannies.

"Of course," smiled Baba. "And I believe we also have some mouse pâté, Low."

"Amazing!" Low grinned.

"That's disgusting." Avery rumpled her nose. How had she not noticed that her best friend was part-owl before now?

Low shrugged. "I can't seem to help myself."

"Here we are," announced Baba, ushering them through a small door off the passageway and into a round room lined from floor to ceiling with wooden drawers of all shapes and sizes. The drawers were a rich mahogany colour, lacquered with layers of varnish. Each one had a hand-written paper label in a small brass frame screwed to it.

Curious, Avery read a row of labels aloud: "'Loch Ness Monster – disguises', 'Leon Felis – miscellaneous', 'Forgotten passwords', 'Morool – spare eyes'." What funny titles. She stopped and turned away, a little disappointed. She had hoped to match the handwriting on the labels with that of the parcels as proof that one of the witches had sent them, but the writing wasn't the same. Mab had seemed to think it *was* one of them, but she hadn't been happy about it. Avery wondered why.

Suddenly a drawer labelled 'Peabody' started jiggling and vibrating, interrupting Avery's thoughts. What was this place?

"Goodness, no respect for the other occupants," tutted Baba. She gave the drawer a sharp knock and it stilled.

"Now, where were we? Oh yes, you'll need a night light." She opened a drawer at her elbow and pulled out an oil lamp, which she lit with a wave of a finger and passed to Low.

"That's *so* cool!" he grinned, surveying the lamp with amazement as he placed it down. It cast a comforting glow, making the room immediately cosy. Baba opened another drawer.

"This is yours, Avery," she said, plumping up a crisp white pillow. Inside the drawer was a bed made up with a brightly coloured patchwork quilt.

Low gasped with surprise. "Wow! There's a whole bed in there."

"Indeed." Baba looked amused. "And the bathroom is here." She pointed to a tiny drawer on the other side of the room. "The flush sticks, so be sure to give it a good hard yank."

"No way!" Low pulled it open and peered inside. "There's actually a real bathroom in here! What is this place, Baba? What's in the other drawers?"

"This room? Why, this is the Repository." Baba handed Avery some tartan pyjamas.

"And what's the Repository?" asked Avery.

"It's a storage facility, of sorts. People have been leaving their magical bits and pieces here for safekeeping, long before us witches came to live here, and that's a very long time ago indeed. Though I like to think we wear our years well. A touch of magic helps." She gave a small chuckle. "And tonight, I will be leaving you both here. Of course, not everything has been left intentionally. The Repository collects lost property too. Teddy bears forgotten on trains, songs that no one can remember the words to. That sort of thing. There is always a place here for something lost, should one want it. I can't quite recall, but I do believe you once fell into that category, Avery dear. Goodness, why can't I remember?"

Avery stared at Baba. What did she mean? Had her parents lost her? Is that why the witches had promised to take care of her?

"Of course, the Repository isn't reliable," Baba went on. "Not at all. In fact, it's quite temperamental. Sometimes you leave something here and it doesn't trust you to have it back. After all these years I seem to have the knack of it, but do you know, I once placed a particularly splendid pair of slippers in that drawer over there marked 'Statue of Liberty – frilly bloomers', and I never saw them again. Yes, quite temperamental. A bit like Cunningfoot in general I would say. Now, Low." Baba turned to him. "Would you prefer a roost or a bed?"

"I think a bed, please," replied Low.

"Then this one should do for you." Baba pulled out another drawer with a duplicate of Avery's bed inside.

"I'll leave you to get changed while I go and prepare some supper," said Baba. "I'll also send word to Bob and Cindy to let them know you're here with us, Avery, and that you're both safe and sound."

Avery was too bewildered to reply, still wondering how she could ever possibly have been lost.

Baba shuffled out of the room, the ball of light she had brought from above the great table bobbing along behind her.

"You know how Baba said that sometimes the drawers don't give things back?" said Low, looking with concern down into the bathroom drawer. "Maybe we shouldn't shut the drawer fully when we use the toilet, just in case."

"Low, do that if it makes you feel better but I honestly think it will be fine. I'd like to know what sorts of secret treasures are in these other drawers." Avery pulled at the handle of one just by her shoulder, curious as to whether some clue about her past might be hidden inside. As the drawer opened a small green claw whipped out, slapped Avery's hand and slammed the drawer shut again.

"Ow!" yelped Avery, rubbing her fingers.

"Curiosity killed the cat," quoted Low with a smirk.

"After the evening we've had, that's not funny," retorted Avery. She sighed, then yawned widely. "I can't wait to get into that bed."

"What a crazy day!" said Low as they both changed and got snug beneath their covers. "Witches, faeries, weird-looking spider people! I'm hoping I might finally get some answers about what I am, too."

Avery looked over at him. "I can't believe you didn't tell me. How long did you say it's been going on?"

"The owl stuff? Only about a year. What was I going to say? I've started sprouting feathers and want to go out hunting at night? Anyway, you can't talk, Cat Girl!" He nodded at her tail. "How long has *that* been happening?"

Avery looked sheepish. "I've actually always known. I'm the last of the Cat Fae – part cat, part human. Bob and Cindy told me that the Cat Fae were an ancient people who had their roots in Persia before they came to Britain a long time ago. Their magic runs through me, even now. But over the years, they've all but disappeared; no one knows why. Bob and Cindy told me about a prophecy that means the Cat Fae can't fail, though I don't understand it…"

Baba spoke the ancient words softly as she came back into the room:

"Tale bites tale, pierced heart,
family bonds and corrupted arts,
Flame-red hair, kindles bad,
rodent-hearted and power-mad,
Memories lost, dark loch,
hidden path 'neath city rock,
Magic man, youth reborn,
preserved awhile by Cat Fae lore,
Hearts bond, hearts weep,
hearts told and histories keep,
Forgotten beast, foot to claw,
airborne, the Great Wyrm's flaw,
Tales stolen, tales remade,
by a tale told, a history's paid.

"I've always liked that one," she went on. "The wizard Magnus Currach found it, I believe. It's written in

The Book of Bells. You can see it for yourselves if you ever visit the island of Iona. The book is kept in the abbey there." She handed Avery a mug of warm milk, and a plate of pâté and toast to Low.

"Do you know what it means?" asked Avery hopefully.

"No, child. That's the thing with prophecies – they just sound like a load of old nonsense until they actually come to pass."

Avery nodded, disappointed. "What was all that about in there with that boy Ghilli?" she asked, sipping her milk.

Baba opened a drawer and pulled out a small stool. She eased herself down, sighing. "We're in a season of darkness, Avery. Magic has been wearing thin in Scotland for some years now, though nobody knows why. Beings like dear Low here are becoming extinct as they're squeezed to the margins of existence. It's in such a time as this that those with wicked intentions would push for power."

"Ghilli's not at all what I imagined a faery to look like," said Low, munching his toast. "And the same things that attacked Avery also attacked the faeries?"

"Yes." Baba nodded slowly. "Though it's unheard of for the Badoch to reach as far south as you and Avery were. Scotland's magic is all out of balance and in my weary old heart I know there's wickedness at work. There's something there, on the tip of my tongue, a fragment of a memory. If only I could remember what it was..." Baba tapped her temple and frowned. "My old brain doesn't work like it used to."

"But we're safe now aren't we, Baba? You and the other witches will take care of us. We can stay here with you," said Avery.

"No, my dear," replied Baba, taking Avery's empty cup and stroking her hand. "It's not safe for you here. Tomorrow you'll journey on. I've someone in mind who'll keep good watch over you until we can make a more permanent arrangement."

Avery hadn't expected this. Her mind still teemed with questions about her past. If she and Low were being sent away it was now or never: she had to ask. "Baba, Bob and Cindy didn't know what happened to my parents. They thought they were dead, but... you just said I was lost. Did my parents leave me here?"

Baba looked at Avery. "Avery dear, Bob and Cindy were right: you are the last of the Cat Fae."

"What happened, Baba?"

"Well..." Baba's voice trailed away and she frowned. "I can't seem to recall. I remember there was such a kerfuffle when you arrived, and there was no doubt as to who you were, not with a tail like that. But other than that... oh dear, I don't know what's wrong with me today..."

"You really can't remember anything?"

Baba shook her head. "I can't think how I can have forgotten..."

"And what about me?" asked Low.

"Well yes, you'll have to go too." Baba patted Low's pillow for him to put his head down. "But I'll send word to your parents so they don't worry.

"Now, both of you, it's time to sleep. You've had a long day. I'll fetch you some proper clothes in the morning. We can't have you wandering around in those Halloween costumes, however apt they may be!"

Baba turned for the door.

"Ah, one moment, I nearly forgot this." She pulled the peach stone out of her pocket, still wrapped up in the handkerchief, and placed it in Avery's hand. "You need to take better care of that. It's full of strong magic; I can feel it. Don't go waving it around like you did back there. It isn't just for anyone – that's why it burned Mab's hand. It was meant only for you."

Avery looked down at the peach stone. If her parents were definitely gone then it *had* to have been one of the witches who sent it.

"Mab didn't know what it was, did she, Baba? Did you send it to me?" Avery asked hopefully.

But Baba shook her head. "No dear, it wasn't me." She smiled, then scrunched up her face. "Oh, but there's something in the back of my mind, if only I could remember…" She tutted. "Never mind, must be my age. Hundreds of years take their toll you know! Goodnight both of you."

With that Baba waved at the oil lamp, which dimmed, then she softly closed the door behind her.

Later that night Avery woke with a start. A terrible wailing ricocheted off the walls, battering her eardrums. She stuffed her fingers in her ears.

"Low, what *is* that noise?" she called out, looking over to his bed. But Low wasn't there. The covers were thrown back and he was gone.

Avery leapt up in panic. Outside in the passage the air pulsed with the awful noise. A smell like singed hair stung Avery's nostrils. She covered her mouth and nose with her sleeve, then followed the screaming sound through the dark corridors back to Cunningfoot's study.

The balls of light now hung stationary above the table, dimmed low, and the ornate chairs were pushed back, as if their inhabitants had leapt up in a hurry. The room was empty except for the hunched figure of Low, peering uncertainly through the entry way and the front door, out of the cupboard into the library.

"Low!" Avery yelled to be heard above the din.

He jumped at the sound of her voice.

"What's this noise? Did you do something?" she demanded, joining him to peer past the coats and boots.

"Me?" He looked insulted. He had a book grasped in each hand.

Avery read one of titles. *"Hoolets and their Habits."*

"I couldn't sleep, y'know, it being night and me being an owl and all, and I kept thinking about the library being *right there* full of all those books, so I came to see if I could find one about me being a Hoolet. I found this other great one about mythical Scottish creatures too..." He trailed off, holding out the second book.

Avery folded her arms across her chest. She wasn't impressed he'd gone exploring without her.

"But anyway," continued Low, scrunching his nose to stop his glasses falling off, "something's happening in the library. I think the books are in pain. Feel this."

He placed Avery's palm on the cover of the book. It seemed to throb and tremble, like a living creature in distress. It was almost as if Avery could feel its panic.

"Come on," she said. "Let's find out what's going on."

Leaving the stationery cupboard, they jogged between the bookshelves, the noise growing louder as they went. Up ahead they could see that a cluster of the library's lights were on. They headed towards them until they emerged into a clearing and found themselves shoulder to shoulder with Kikimora and Baba.

"Stand back, both of you," commanded Baba. "What are you doing here?"

"We were woken by the noise," replied Avery. She looked down in horror. "What is that?"

At their feet lay a large blackened casket with ornate iron carrying handles at either end. Strong leather straps bolted to the casket by brass pins were thrown back and the remnants of a heavy lock, which had been prised open, hung in shattered pieces. The casket's lid had been smashed and thick smoke billowed from inside, carrying the hideous burning smell to the far corners of the library. This was where the screaming was coming from.

At the bottom of the casket, Avery could just about make out the outline of a charred book, slowly disintegrating as it smouldered. Out of its cover protruded the handle of a knife.

"*The Life and Times of Whimbrel Baxter and L—*" read Avery. The rest of the title had been burned away.

Baba held Avery closely to her side. "It's dying, the poor thing. By the looks of it, it's been murdered."

Avery pulled herself away from Baba. "Well don't just stand there, do something!"

"There's nothing we can do." Kikimora shook her head sadly. "There must have been a powerful story in that book for someone to want to kill it."

"Or a terrible secret," added Baba.

"Either way. We'll never know," said Kikimora. "It's gone out of all knowledge now. The magic in that knife means every copy of that book that exists throughout the world will have died too."

"We can at least offer it some comfort, surely?" protested Avery, stooping to reach into the casket.

Avery's arm brushed the edge, and in an instant, the lights of the library went out and the smoke vanished. Everything was plunged into darkness, until a soft glow began to grow.

Only a few feet away from where she knelt, Avery could see Mab huddled over one of the bookshelves. What was going on? Mab hadn't been there a second ago. Avery looked around her. And where had the others gone? They had vanished too. Avery felt panic rising up inside her.

Underneath her fingers she could still feel the rough burnt edge of the casket, but when she looked down there was nothing there. Avery jumped when Mab glanced hurriedly over her shoulder, but the witch looked right through her, as if Avery wasn't there. Avery frowned, pinching the back of her hand. "Why can't she see me? What is she doing?" she wondered.

Whatever it was, Mab obviously didn't want to be caught doing it. Avery followed the witch's furtive movements to the shelf.

The casket!

Mab was pulling it out from a hiding place on a bookshelf, and it was perfectly intact. Avery shook her head. Was she seeing something that had already happened? Something from before the casket had been destroyed? Suddenly it all added up in Avery's mind with a sickening jolt. Could it have been Mab who had murdered the book?

Avery jumped at the touch of a hand on her arm.

"No dear, don't touch it. There's great evil at work here. That knife must be dealt with correctly. This is a job for Ceridwen. She's an expert at disposals." Baba's voice floated towards Avery before the library reappeared properly, the lights back on. Mab was nowhere to be seen.

Avery withdrew her hand from the casket in alarm. She felt dizzy. What had just happened? It was as though the present had vanished and she had been able to see a vision from the past.

Suddenly the wailing stopped. The silence was almost painful as the final pieces of the murdered book crinkled away with a hiss. All that remained was ashes. The knife toppled onto its side on the floor, and the casket collapsed into a heap of burnt splinters.

Mab's sharp voice rang out across the library. "This way, Ceridwen!"

Mab swept into the space, followed by the other witch. It might have been Ceridwen, but it was impossible to really tell. She wore a long leather tunic, thick leather gloves that reached all the way up to her shoulders and a metal can over her head with a narrow slit for her eyes.

She held up an enormous pair of tongs, which she carried at arm's length as she advanced on the murderous knife.

Mab stopped short when she saw Avery and Low. She glowered at them.

"What are *you* doing here?" she asked.

"W-w-we woke with the noise," stammered Avery.

"You should be in bed. It isn't safe." Mab raised her monocle. "There is a book murderer at large! Come, Ceridwen! We must not delay. The cauldron is prepared. The broth we've conjured should be strong enough to deal with the magic in this weapon."

Ceridwen had just managed to get hold of the knife with the tongs when a terrific thudding sound caused her to lose her grip and it clattered to the floor again. Into the clearing galloped Glaurt, followed by a flustered-looking Edgar.

"The north door is secure, Miss Mab. Nothing got in that way and certainly nothing is getting out." Edgar clutched at his waistcoat and bowed repeatedly.

"Nothing!" added Glaurt, shaking his head enthusiastically and beaming at Avery.

Hot on the heels of Glaurt and Edgar were Lilith and Jezebel. Jezebel's tower of blue hair leaned dangerously to one side, her face flushed. They had obviously been running.

"Ze west entrance is secure," Lilith panted.

"I can't say the same for the east door." Cassandra's sweet voice was filled with distress as she too joined them. She held up a gilded lock and a door handle, splintered wood protruding nastily from three of its sides. "Someone got in there and I'm pretty sure they went out there too. I've secured it with a holding spell for now," she added.

Mab tutted. "Come, Ceridwen. I want that thing destroyed. And I want those two back in bed." She glared at Avery and Low. "Immediately."

"I quite agree," added Baba, clapping her hands together and gently ushering them around the bookshelves and back towards the cupboard. "Goodnight all!"

The three of them returned to the Repository in silence. After Baba had tucked them into their beds, she waved a hand over them both and softly said, "It's time for sleep for two weary souls. Rest well and arise refreshed in the morning."

Baba paused outside in the passage and considered the closed door. Running a glowing finger around the frame she murmured, "Keep them safe, door. You are only to open for the smell of breakfast."

Nodding with satisfaction, she flapped off down the passage, tapping her temple and muttering, "Deary me, Whimbrel Baxter, now that name does ring a bell. If only I could remember…"

On the other side of the door, Avery and Low whispered to each other in the dim lamplight.

"What happened to you back there, Avery?" asked Low. "You just froze, it was like you'd seen a ghost or something. I don't think anyone noticed but me."

"Low, I had some kind of vision when I touched the side of the casket. Everything disappeared and I saw Mab pulling it out from the shelf." Avery felt like she wanted to cry. Her head ached with all of the questions buzzing round her brain. "I think it was Mab who murdered that book! She must have tried to cover it up by making it look like an intruder had come in through the east door of the library."

"But why would she do that?" asked Low.

Avery sighed. "I have no idea."

They both lay still in stunned silence, until Baba's spell slowly worked its magic and they drifted off to sleep.

7

The next morning Low sat up in bed and sniffed the air. "Eggs!" he declared cheerfully. "Avery, I can smell eggs!"

Watery sunshine trickled in from a small skylight high above them. Avery yawned and uncurled herself as Low flopped out of bed and waddled to the door. On the floor outside sat a tray laden with hot buttered toast, fried eggs and sweet tea. Two neat piles of clothes sat either side.

"Clean clothes and breakfast!" announced Low, carrying the tray triumphantly back into the room and laying it down. Avery crept out of her drawer to join him and they sat cross-legged, contentedly demolishing the tray's contents.

When they were both dressed, they peeked out into the passage. All was quiet.

"Maybe everyone's still in bed?" ventured Low.

Earthen passages dotted with wooden doors of all sorts of shapes and sizes wound off in different directions.

"This place is a warren," said Low, shaking his head as he looked around. He stopped and Avery bumped into him.

"What's wrong?"

"Nothing, just saw a rat scurrying off." He frowned.

"Ugh, rats." Avery shuddered. "They obviously need to work on their housekeeping spells around here. Cindy would be outraged."

After a few wrong turns they found their way back to the study. Cassandra stood at the long table, sifting through a sheaf of papers.

"Goodness, are you two okay? That was quite a night we had." The witch's pale face was full of concern. "Why don't you go out for a walk while you wait for the others to get up? It's a beautiful morning and it would be lovely for you to see a bit of Edinburgh while you're here."

Avery closed her eyes. Her head still ached. The thought of warm sunshine on her face was too tempting. "Is that okay?" she asked. "I mean, is it safe?"

"I would have thought a bit of fresh air would be just the thing after last night. In fact, you should head in the direction of Canonmills," said Cassandra, looking pointedly at Avery. "It's a fine walk, with views of the sea. Keep the castle on your left and aim for the river. You can't go wrong."

Avery tried to read Cassandra's expression but couldn't. *Canonmills.* That name rang a bell.

When they stepped through the cupboard, the library was open but its human inhabitants seemed oblivious to the presence of the witches' house. A man wearing a red bow tie and a staff ID badge scratched his head as he examined Gluart's splintered book trolley. "Now how has that happened?" he muttered to himself.

Downstairs, Edgar had nestled himself in a dark recess above the Reception desk. He scuttled down when he saw them. "Good morning, good morning, off out are we? Not a good idea, not a good idea." Edgar blinked his many eyes at them, wringing his three pairs of hairy hands anxiously.

Avery placed her fingertips on her throbbing temples. Her headache was getting worse. "I could really do with some fresh air, Edgar. Cassandra suggested we go for a walk."

"Did she? Did she? Well now, Mab has said no one should leave."

Avery gritted her teeth. Mab was a liar and a book murderer, so if she'd said they shouldn't leave then there was no way Avery was staying put. She glowered at Edgar and shoved her hands in her pockets, her fingers brushing the objects nestled there. The guidebook. Of course! How could she have forgotten? *Canonmills – Past and Present. A Traveller's Guide.*

She pulled it out. Suddenly Cassandra's pointed look made sense. Of all the places she might have suggested, Cassandra had chosen the very place that matched the little book – she must be hinting that it was *her* who had sent the objects. It was Cassandra who had saved Avery's life by sending her the peach stone.

"Avery, are you okay?" asked Low. "What's that?" He nodded at the book in her hand.

"I can't explain here," she whispered, giving him a meaningful look.

Low took the hint. "So Edgar…" He grasped the spider's shoulder and turned him towards the desk where the receptionists were busily working away. "I still don't understand this magical realm business. Tell me again why the people in the library can't see us?"

"Well, it's like this." Edgar wriggled his whiskers. "The magical realm exists in the in-between spaces, the corner of your eye and so on…"

Avery smiled to herself and slipped out the library door.

Minutes later Low joined her.

"Good distraction," she laughed.

Low laughed too.

It felt good to be outside and Avery's headache started to ease. The day was cold but bright, and the pavement was already full of people going about their morning business. Nobody seemed to notice the giant black stallion tethered to one of the lamp posts outside the library. Ghilli stood at its nose, making preparations to leave.

"Ah." He bowed. "I didn't recognise you when I saw you last night, Avery. It's good to see you again."

"You know me?" asked Avery in surprise. How could Ghilli know her and she not remember him? He was only a little older than Avery herself. It didn't make any sense.

"Everyone here knows Avery and she doesn't recognise any of them," explained Low.

The faery nodded thoughtfully. "I'm afraid I have to leave, but I'm sorry I haven't had the opportunity to get to know you, Low, and spend some time with you, Avery. I must return to Inchmahome with news that the witches have agreed to help us." His expression darkened. "Edgar told me about last night's events. I slept in the stables with Kest here, so didn't know anything of it until this morning. Very nasty."

He reached up to grab hold of his horse's bridle but paused, fixing Avery and Low with a long look. "If you ever need anything, either of you, you should know the faeries of Inchmahome are at your service."

"Er, thanks," said Avery, hoping she'd never have to call on such a serious offer. "I hope you find out what's behind the Badoch attacks."

Ghilli winked at them both and flashed a smile, before leaping onto Kest's back and charging off down the road.

"Did you see that?" squealed Low, pulling on Avery's sleeve in his excitement. The faery stallion had galloped off through the oblivious crowds and up into the sky. "Ghilli's so cool!"

"Kest was the one who was flying," replied Avery with an amused roll of her eyes.

Avery and Low were soon mingling with commuters and tourists on Edinburgh's Royal Mile, the castle seeming to keep watch on them as it crouched above on its steep rock.

"What was going on back there when we were talking to Edgar? You didn't look right at all," said Low.

Avery handed him the guidebook.

"'*Canonmills – Past and Present*,'" he read aloud, opening the little book up. The paper was dry and crisp, stained yellow with age. "Isn't that the same place Cassandra said we should go?"

Avery nodded.

Low scanned the guide. It was slightly torn along the creases where it had been folded and re-folded over the years. "It sounds nice. It says that there's a loch with ducks and you can hire a rowing boat. Where did you get it?"

"It came in the post a few weeks ago, wrapped up in brown paper. No note or anything." Avery reached into her pocket and pulled out the other objects she had received. "These came in the same way. The peach stone arrived last of all."

Low stopped. He took the piece of sea glass and held it up to the light.

"A while ago I started feeling like I was being watched," said Avery. "Now I know it was the Badoch. These things started to arrive around the same time."

"Did you know there's something engraved on this glass?" asked Low, squinting at it. "Underneath the frostiness. I can't see what it is."

"Where?" Avery took the object from him. Low was right, there was something there, but she couldn't make it out.

"It's funny that Cassandra suggested we should go to Canonmills, isn't it?" said Low.

"I think so too. She gave me the strangest look back there. I'm sure she was trying to tell me she's the one who's been sending me these things." Avery dropped the sea glass back into her pocket.

"So, do you want to go?" Low asked.

"Where?"

"Canonmills. Look at the map." Low pointed at the little book. "We're here, there's the castle and we need to go…" He turned the guidebook around a few times before concluding, "…this way."

"Yeah, come on."

They walked down the busy street, and Low scratched his head. "I don't get why Cassandra wouldn't say it outright. Why didn't she just tell you she'd sent the guide?"

"You saw Mab's reaction when we first arrived," said Avery. "She wasn't happy to see me at all. And she looked like she might explode when I suggested one of the witches must have sent the peach stone to help me. Cassandra must have done it without Mab knowing. If only I could check whether her handwriting is the same as on the packages, I would know for sure."

Avery skipped down some stone steps and turned to face Low. "And what if there's more to it than that? I told you what I saw in the library last night – Mab taking the casket from the shelf. She murdered that book and then covered it up." She paused. "Low, what if Mab isn't a good witch?"

He frowned. "What do you mean?"

"Well, what if Mab set the Badoch on me? Baba said how unusual it was for them to be so far south. What if she's got something to do with the attacks on the faeries too? Ghilli certainly thought she was covering it up. Maybe Cassandra has found out what Mab is doing and is secretly trying to stop her?"

Low shook his head and pushed past her down the steps. "That doesn't make any sense. Why would Mab want to attack you? She's one of the people sworn to protect you, remember."

Avery followed him. "I don't know. Maybe it's got something to do with the prophecy. Maybe she wants the Cat Fae to fail."

"Look, I get Mab's scary and all but it seems a bit far-fetched to me."

"Well I don't trust her." Avery persisted as they waited for a moment at a crossing packed with shoppers.

"If it was Cassandra who sent this guidebook she wasn't the first person to have it. Look." Low pointed to the back cover. In faint pencil, so faded that it was hard to make out, someone had printed their name: *A. BAXTER.*

"It's old." Avery was dismissive. "I'm sure it's belonged to lots of people."

But Low wasn't listening. "Is this Scotland Street?" He squinted as he looked for a sign. They had come out at the top of a steep road, which dropped away to a perfect sea view framed by the grand Georgian buildings of Edinburgh's New Town.

"'Edinburgh's New Town was built between 1765 and 1850 to relieve overcrowding around the castle,'" quoted Low from the book. "And – weird – under this street there's an old railway tunnel. It says here the train used to be pulled on ropes!" Low chuckled, pleased with this nugget of information.

Avery stopped. "Wouldn't it be cool if we could

get into the tunnel?" she said, keen for a distraction from her thoughts about Mab. "I wonder if there's an entrance."

"Stop right there," demanded Low. "No, it wouldn't be *cool*! After all that's happened in the last twenty-four hours I'm not going in any creepy old tunnel. I'm staying right here in the sunshine. What? What have you seen?"

Avery had suddenly frozen, her eyes fixed on something over Low's shoulder. The smile slid from her face.

"Shhh, don't say anything and don't look behind you," she replied. "Is Canonmills this way?"

"Yes, down here, through the park," said Low, trying to peek out of the corner of his eye.

"Stop looking!" hissed Avery. "We're being followed!"

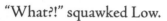

"What?!" squawked Low.

"There's a strange woman over there in a long coat and big brown boots," whispered Avery, "and I'm sure she's following us. She was up near the castle and now she's here. She keeps looking at us."

"Quick, down there." Low pointed to a path that trickled down a tree-covered bank and though a pretty park. "We might lose her."

They followed the path until it dipped out of sight of the road, then they ran across the park. Panting, they stopped at a pair of iron gates.

"Can you see her?" huffed Low, hands on his knees.

"No, I think we lost her. She's probably one of Mab's minions." Avery scowled.

"Well, whoever she is, this is Canonmills," announced Low.

On the opposite side of the street stood a stone building several storeys high. Little white framed windows dotted its walls.

"A long time ago it used to be a mill. Round here should be the mill wheel and the loch," said Low, consulting the guide.

They wandered on before turning left at a busy crossroads, finding themselves on the forecourt of a petrol station, the pumps chugging as customers filled their cars.

"That's odd," said Low, turning the guide around in confusion. "Where's the loch, and the ducks?"

Avery raised an eyebrow. "Not here any more. That guide must be pretty out of date. Hey, look at this." She patted a stone set in the wall of the petrol station kiosk. It was much older than the bricks around it and was fractured by a large crack. Engraved on it were letters in a scrawling script, worn faint by time. Avery traced her fingers over the words:

At that moment the sun went in. Avery glanced up. Thick rain clouds glowered over the rooftops and a chill breeze caught at her hair.

"Is it me or do we keep bumping into the name Baxter?" asked Low, nervously looking up at the sky too.

"Yes." Avery nodded slowly. "The murdered book was about a Whimbrel Baxter. That guide has the name A. Baxter written in it. Now this stone. I don't like it. I think we should head back to the library."

"Me too," agreed Low.

They hurried back towards the park, the sky darkening with each step. As they rounded the corner, who should be standing between the park's iron gates but the woman in the long brown coat and big brown boots. Lank grey hair trailed down to her waist and she stared out at them with hollow grey eyes.

"Oh dear, dear, dear," muttered Low. "This is bad. I can feel it."

"Come on," said Avery, taking his hand and trying to sound braver than she felt. "We've got away from worse than her before."

But as they drew closer, they saw that the woman was trembling from head to toe. She was more scared than they were.

"P-p-please." She approached, arm outstretched. "D-d-don't go through the park. You have to *ask* me." She glanced around. "Th-th-they are coming. There isn't much time. *He* knows." The woman nodded at Low.

"Me? Wh-wh-what do I know?" stammered Low.

"You read about me. In the library." The woman fixed Low with a pleading look. "But I can't tell you. You have to *ask*. Please hurry. *They* are coming!"

"What is this all about?" asked Avery, looking between Low and the woman.

"I don't..." Low faltered. "Hang on, I *did* read about you, last night when I was looking for a book on Hoolets!"

"Yes, yes!" The woman pulled at his arm.

"The clothes, the hair: you're Bean Nighe!" exclaimed Low.

"Bean what?" said Avery, looking baffled.

"She's a Scottish mythical creature," explained Low. "Although obviously not that mythical, because she's here."

"No time, no time!" begged the woman.

"In legend, she asks you three riddles, and if you get them right then you can ask her three questions," continued Low.

"What's so amazing about that?" asked Avery.

"Think about it. We could ask her anything. Anything at all! I can find out more about this Hoolet thing and you can find out if Mab is the one who's after you."

Avery's eyes drifted to the horizon as questions jostled for attention in her mind.

"Right, here goes." Low cleared his throat. "Bean Nighe, what is your first riddle?"

She beckoned them closer and they bent near to hear.

"I have fur, but I'm not a coat.
I have a tail, but I'm not a kite.
I have nine lives, but I'm not immortal.
I belong with a witch,
And in stories old,
With cauldron and broomstick.
Who am I?"

Avery and Low turned to each other with matching confused expressions.

"We've met several witches now. We should know this," said Avery.

"I'm not sure any of them are like any witch I've ever read about, though," replied Low.

"They all live together at Cunningfoot, so maybe that's it. A witch's companion is another witch," offered Avery hopefully.

"No wait," said Low to Bean Nighe. "That's not our final answer." He rubbed his chin thoughtfully. "It's something with fur and a tail; that's what the riddle says. Well, Cassandra has a rat."

"She does?" exclaimed Avery in astonishment.

"Oh yes." Low tapped his nose. "I can always smell rodents. I smelt it when we met her last night. She hides it under her hair and talks to it when no one's looking. I've seen it a couple of times too; I think it was the rat I saw outside our door this morning."

"So that's it then, a rat," said Avery.

"No, no, hang on!" Low jumped in again. "The riddle says, 'in stories old'. I mean, have you seen any of the witches we know carrying a broomstick?" Low repeated the riddle to himself again slowly. "'I have nine lives…' That's it!"

"What?" demanded Avery.

"Fur, a tail, nine lives, and in old stories witches always have one. It's a cat!" Low jumped up and down in excitement and turned to Bean Nighe. A tiny wisp of a smile flitted across her careworn face.

Bean Nighe beckoned them close again.

"*Seven magical clans of Scotland,*
Baxter, Brodich, Lammermuir, Lennox,
Marra, Currach and Logan.
Powers passed from generation to generation.
If my magical daughter is a witch,
What is my magical son?"

"Seven magical clans of Scotland. How interesting," mused Low, momentarily distracted.

"Low, will you focus?" Avery snapped. "A magical girl is called a witch, so a magical son would be a wizard, right?"

Bean Nighe nodded, then beckoned them close a final time.

"*I beat a rhythm, but I'm not a drum.*
I race but never win.

Encased in flesh and bone,
I may be given but never sold.
Great power I wield, but what is strength to one,
Is weakness to another."

"'I beat a rhythm…'" repeated Low.

"'Encased in flesh and bone', so it's part of a person's body?" Avery guessed.

"I think you're onto something," said Low, clicking his fingers.

"What about a heart," cried Avery, gripping Low's arm in her excitement. "A heart pumps and races. When you love someone, people talk of giving their heart away. Do you think that's it?"

"It's a good guess. I don't get the bit about it being strength to one and weakness to another, but I can't think of anything else." Low shrugged.

They turned to Bean Nighe.

"A heart," said Avery.

Bean Nighe shuddered and glanced behind her again. "Yes. Now quickly ask me your questions. They are coming!"

"Avery, I've just remembered something else I read last night," said Low urgently. "Bean Nighe usually appears just before something awful happens."

"You don't have to tell me," replied Avery. "The hairs on my neck stood up when she shuddered just now. And I know exactly who's coming. It's the Badoch!"

"Let's just go!" exclaimed Low.

"No!" pleaded Bean Nighe. "You r̶ ̶
been sent to you and you must ask m̶

"Sent? By who?" Avery stared a̶ ̶
this why Cassandra wanted them to come to Canonmills?
To meet Bean Nighe?

Low grabbed her arm. "Wait! Is that what you want to
ask?" Avery ran her hands through her hair, thinking of
her parents, the prophecy, Mab. "I don't know!" she cried.
"There are so many questions I need answers to – I can't
choose!"

Low blinked rapidly, as if trying to catch a fleeing
thought. "The things she asked us are clues. I'm sure they
are. We need to ask about those things."

"Yes, yes!" Bean Nighe nodded. She was shaking so
violently now that she was barely able to get the words out.

"Okay," said Avery, forcing herself to be calm. "Well,
the answer to the first question was a cat. In the old stories
a cat accompanies a witch, but none of the witches we've
met have cats as far as we know."

"You're part cat, Avery. Maybe that's it, maybe we need
to ask about you and the witches?" Low ventured, but
Avery shook her head.

"How does the wizard fit in then? Or the heart? There
must be a connection, Low. I wonder… Everyone at
Cunningfoot knew me but I didn't know them. Bob and

dy could never answer my questions about the Cat Fae. I mean, maybe I do accompany a witch but I never knew."

Low sighed. "That still doesn't explain the wizard and heart answers."

"Please hurry," pleaded Bean Nighe.

"Oh, this is no good. I can't think under pressure!" cried Avery. "I don't know, I could be a wizard's companion for all I know!" She scuffed her boots on the path in frustration. She didn't notice the look Bean Nighe gave her, but Low did.

"That's it! You're not a witch's cat, you're a wizard's!" he said urgently. "Bean Nighe, who is Avery's wizard?"

They could hardly hear Bean Nighe's trembling voice over the rising wind. Leaves scuttered across the pavement.

"Acton Baxter the magic man is your wizard!"

Avery took a step backwards, eyes wide. "Acton Baxter? A. Baxter… And where is he, Bean Nighe?"

On the edge of her vision Avery could see shadowy figures rising out of the dark corners of the park. The Badoch. She tried to push away her dread. Low was beside himself with panic, repeatedly adjusting his glasses and hopping from foot to foot.

"He is lost," wailed Bean Nighe. "He cannot die while you live. You must live and you must find him!"

Avery grabbed Bean Nighe's hands. "And how do we live, Bean Nighe? How can we escape the Badoch right now?"

Bean Nighe raised a long grey finger and pointed to a large black hole framed in stone underneath the path down which they had first run. It was so overhung with shrubs that they hadn't seen it.

"Into the old railway tunnel!" directed Bean Nighe, her voice cracking.

Low looked horrified. "In there?"

"Come with us, Bean Nighe!" insisted Avery.

She shook her head. "They will not follow you into the tunnel. They are afraid of the sleeping creature. Beware the Crannog!" Bean Nighe's voice broke into a terrible scream. She clutched her face with her hands and then vanished on the wind.

The Badoch suddenly seemed to be everywhere, their long shadowy arms reaching out as Avery and Low scrambled backwards. Their eager hissing thrummed through Avery's bones.

"We're not going to make it!" shouted Low, eyes wide with terror as sharp black claws gripped his arm tight.

9

"Yes, we are!" Avery shouted back. Every inch of her skin prickled with determination as she grabbed Low's other arm and pulled, freeing him from the Badoch's grip.

Then she began to run.

The short distance to the mouth of the railway tunnel seemed to lengthen like a telescope, but Avery gritted her teeth, pouring every ounce of energy into her muscles. The sky had turned the colour of an ash pit. It was nearly impossible to tell what was solid ground for the writhing mass of surging shadows that filled the park. Dimly aware of strong claws grabbing at her limbs, Avery focused on the tunnel entrance. The Badoch hadn't caught her at the school disco, and there was no way she was going to let them catch her here.

Twisting her body, she mustered all of her cat-like abilities and leapt just out of reach, pulling Low with her. Then they were inside, backs flat against the wall of the tunnel.

Low whimpered as dark figures crowded out the

daylight from the tunnel mouth. They could hear them snarling and scrabbling at the stone.

"We need to go further in!" cried Avery.

"B-b-b-but what about the sleeping creature Bean Nighe mentioned?" protested Low. "We don't even know what it is! If the Badoch are scared of it, it must be bad."

The tunnel was steep, the floor rough and uneven. Low slipped and fell. "My glasses!"

Avery felt around in the dust at their feet until she found the metal frames. "Here you go. Let's stop a minute and let our eyes get used to the dark. We've both got good night sight so we'll be able to see just fine in a minute."

"That was so close, Avery! I think I'm going to be sick…"

"Yes, it was," replied Avery quietly. "And the only reason you're in this danger is because of me. We'll follow this tunnel to the main railway station, then when we're back at the library we'll get the witches to send you home."

Low was outraged. "You will not!" he declared, putting his glasses back on with a huff. "You're my best friend, Avery, I'm not going anywhere! And besides, we need to find this wizard of yours."

Avery looked at her friend through the darkness, then threw her arms around him in a fierce hug. "Thanks, Low."

Low shuffled awkwardly. "Well now," he muttered, rubbing some imaginary dirt from his sleeves.

Avery smiled to herself and they turned back to the path.

"I guess we just keep following the tunnel," said Avery, putting her hand out to steady herself on the wall. Within a split second, the light in the tunnel changed.

A flickering glow coming from somewhere behind her caught the rough edges of the walls. She couldn't see Low any more but she could hear him calling. He sounded far away.

"Avery? Avery? Are you okay?" To Low, it was like someone had pressed pause on his best friend. Avery had stopped, stock-still, her eyes staring blankly into the darkness. "You've frozen again. Oh dear, I don't like this."

Avery, meanwhile, could feel the rough wall of the tunnel under her hand, but the air seemed different. It felt just like the vision she had had in the library last night.

She looked about her. The flickering glow was that of candlelight. It was coming from a small side tunnel. Edging closer, Avery saw two young people facing each other in the cramped space.

A tall red-haired teen had her back to Avery. She was talking animatedly to an even taller young man, with broad shoulders, sun-kissed skin and short hair the colour of caramel. He faced Avery, so she could see him clearly.

He wore a navy waistcoat with white lines embroidered across it in strange geometric patterns, and his shirtsleeves were rolled up. Avery had an odd feeling of certainty that he hated having things flapping around his wrists. Likewise, the red woollen scarf wrapped around his neck gave Avery a jolt of familiarity. She knew that the small white dots running along the edge were actually a pattern of mice knitted into the scarf, though there was no way she could see that from where she stood.

The young man's bright blue eyes flickered to Avery over the girl's shoulder. Avery didn't think he could see her, but it was as if he knew she was there. She felt a comforting sense of recognition, like unexpectedly seeing a friend's face in a crowd, or finding a beloved old teddy at the back of the wardrobe.

"Acton, join me!" insisted the girl. She raised her arm and the flame of the candle floating above her shoulder flickered with the movement.

Avery's jaw dropped. Acton? Her wizard? What was he doing here? And who was this girl? Avery peered closer, before she realised that the red hair was familiar, even just from behind.

It was Mab. A young Mab. Avery was certain of it.

"Join me, my love, and share the destiny of the Logans." Her voice was eager, excited. "Let us put our families' feud behind us forever. Whimbrel Baxter was a fool in thwarting my own dear papa's plans, but we shall remedy that! Acton, my love, you see what your father could not. We shall wake the Crannog together and harness its great power. All the earth will submit to our will!"

Acton looked horrified. "Listen to yourself. This is madness! The Crannogs were wiped out for a reason – they were capable of only death and destruction." He shook his head. "This beast has been asleep for thousands of years, and it must stay that way. Wake it and it will ravage the world!"

"You are wrong! If you could only see!" cried Mab, reaching out towards him. "Whimbrel discovered how to wake the Crannog. You are his son, he trusts you – you can steal the secret from him."

Acton backed away and Avery caught the sound of running water, rapidly growing louder until the tunnel echoed with the noise of a thundering torrent. Mab shook her head frantically. "What is this, Acton? What is this treachery?"

"Your father will always be the same scheming Crux Logan of old," shouted Acton. "My father won this land from him in a fair duel, and I will not permit that monster to be woken. As we speak, the Canonmills Loch is draining into the cavern where the Crannog sleeps. Every drop of water strengthens the magic that holds it asleep." Acton was defiant. "In years to come, the city will grow over this land, and with each brick the magic will be strengthened again and again. You will not wake that monster!"

Mab screamed. "Traitor! You may have found a way around my father's curse on your family, but I will finish what he started." She leapt at Acton, her hands like claws. Avery was astonished to see that Acton didn't look fearful, or even shocked. It was as if he had expected this to happen.

Blue sparks flew violently from Mab's fingertips like lightning. "Death is what you deserve. You will not thwart me again!"

Acton crumpled under the young witch's magic.

Although she knew there was nothing she could do, Avery couldn't stop herself from crying out.

There was a sudden blinding flash, and then something strange began to happen. It was as though Acton was collapsing in on himself until, with a blinding flash, he vanished.

"I will find a way to undo what you have done, Acton Baxter," Mab spat out as Avery's vision began to fade. "And I will hunt down that precious Cat Fae of yours through all her nine lives so that I may finally destroy you. Once and for all."

10

"Avery! Avery!" called Low. "Are you okay? What did you see?"

Avery felt weak, and her head had started to pound. She blinked, her eyes readjusting to the dark. "I-I-I was over there." She pointed. "There's a side tunnel. I saw two people arguing. One of them was Acton."

"Your wizard!" exclaimed Low.

"Yes," Avery nodded. "There was a girl with him – I couldn't see her face but I think it was Mab, when she was younger. She talked about waking something called a Crannog… and how they would rule together."

"A Crannog?" interrupted Low. "That's the monster Bean Nighe warned us about."

Avery nodded. "Acton was trying to stop Mab. Whimbrel Baxter, the man who wrote the book murdered in the library last night, is Acton's father. He knew how to wake the Crannog and Mab wanted Acton to betray him."

"What? Hang on. I can't keep up," protested Low.

In the dark tunnel, Avery recounted how Acton defied

Mab, drained the loch into the cavern and enchanted the city to keep the monster asleep.

"That must be why the loch isn't up above ground any more," replied Low.

Avery pushed her fingertips into the skin on her forehead. She felt dizzy. "Low, Mab said she was going to hunt me down. She's trying to kill me – this proves it. And she said I've got nine lives. What does that mean?"

"Look, sit down for a minute. You've gone really pale." Low crouched beside Avery as she sank to the ground.

"Low, I've got nine lives and… and I'm a wizard's cat… but he's gone… so I'm not any more, am I?" She was gabbling and she knew it, but Avery couldn't make sense of everything. Worst of all was the ache in her heart. "When I looked at Acton, he was so familiar. Oh Low, for the smallest of moments I felt like… like I'd found what's always been missing. Like I belonged. Does that make sense?" She sniffed. "But he's gone. Mab killed him and now she's after me."

"What did you *actually* see?" asked Low. "Bean Nighe said he wasn't dead, didn't she? She said he couldn't die because of you."

Avery stared at him, struggling to compute his words.

"Well." Avery frowned. "She kind of zapped him. Blue flashes came out of her fingers. He collapsed and then he disappeared. He looked dead, and Mab certainly meant him to be dead. She said that death was what he deserved. But… maybe you're right. What did Bean Nighe say again?"

"She said he was lost, not dead. She said we needed to find him, and that he couldn't die while you lived," repeated Low.

Avery sat up, her face alight. "Do you think Bean Nighe was right, Low? Do you think Mab made a mistake and somehow he didn't die?"

Low nodded. "I do. Bean Nighe said she had been sent. I think someone wants us to find him, Avery!"

"He's not dead. Oh Low, he's not dead!" Avery felt hope flood through her. "And Cassandra must have known all along. She must have sent Bean Nighe. No wonder she's too afraid to say anything if that's what Mab does to people who stand up to her."

"And this thing, the Crannog, Bean Nighe warned us about it, it must still be sleeping down here." Low shivered at the thought.

Avery got to her feet. "Come on, let's look." She walked to the opening in the side tunnel and peered into the darkness.

Low sighed and followed her. "Please, Avery, let's not go down there. Let's just stick to the main tunnel. I can't take any more monsters!"

"Low, we have to see if it's still there," she said, edging her way along the side tunnel. The pitch-black was so dense even Avery's night vision couldn't pierce the gloom. She felt her way forward, shuffling her feet along the dusty floor, one hand on the cold stone wall beside her. Low followed reluctantly.

Suddenly, Avery stopped, causing Low to bump into her with an "Oof!"

"Shhh!" she hissed. "There's a light up ahead."

A faint glow flickered at the end of the side tunnel. They followed it, and found the passageway opened out into an enormous cavern filled with a strange shimmering light. Avery put her finger to her lips and they stopped to listen. When nothing stirred, they stepped out of the tunnel.

Most of the cavern was taken up by a large lake, its surface perfectly still. On it floated the broken remains of some old-fashioned rowing boats. They had once been painted in bright jolly colours, but now the paint peeled from their wooden frames. Rotting cushions were spread on the seats.

"It's the loch from the guidebook. Those boats must have been sucked down with the water," whispered Low.

"No ducks here now," replied Avery. "It's been buried underneath the city."

The roof of the cavern was made up of a jumble of brick arches and pillars, which seemed to be defying gravity. The pillars were cut off in mid-air, high above the water. The brickwork dripped with years of damp and green algae.

"How is this place even staying up?" asked Low, gazing around.

"I'm pretty sure it's magic," said Avery. "Acton said the city would grow over the loch, helping to keep the Crannog asleep."

"Well, where is it?" Low scanned the echoey cavern nervously.

Avery tiptoed to the edge of the lake and peered in. "I'd say it's in there."

Low tiptoed forward too, one arm outstretched so that his fingertips remained in contact with the wall behind him.

The faint light that filled the cavern came from the surface of the water. It glimmered softly, as if a layer of magic sat on top like mist. Looking through the shimmering watery haze, they saw an enormous creature lying beneath.

The monster looked ancient, like something from a forgotten world. Its skin was an oily dark grey. Black barbs ran down its spine, and long muscular limbs ended in huge, powerful claws. Its eyes were thin lashless slits, set either side of a long snout.

"Mab wanted to team up with that?" muttered Low.

Avery shuddered as she looked from the creature's yellowed tusks jutting out of its slack mouth to the two jagged horns protruding from its forehead. It made her skin crawl.

"Is it dead?" Low asked with a whimper.

"No, look, you can see it breathing," whispered Avery, pointing. "Acton said the magic would keep it asleep, and Bean Nighe called it 'the sleeping creature'."

Low clutched Avery's arm. "Well, we should leave it that way. Let's go!"

Avery nodded, but was unable to peel her eyes away from the strange submerged monster.

Low hooked his arm in hers and pulled her back. "I said, let's go!"

They turned and clambered their way back up to the main tunnel, where they stood in shocked silence.

"Mab wanted to wake that thing up so somehow it would help her to have power over everything," said Avery at last. "I thought there was something not right about her, but this seems crazy."

"It does," agreed Low gloomily.

"You do believe me though, Low, don't you? You believe what I saw in my vision?" asked Avery, suddenly anxious.

"Of course!" he replied. "You saw them talking about it and there it was, just like they'd said."

"We need to get out of this tunnel," said Avery urgently. "We need to go to Cassandra. She must have a plan for finding Acton. There must be a way that she can help us without Mab finding out." She turned and began striding up the main tunnel, away from Canonmills.

Low struggled to catch up. "We'll have to be careful. What if some of the other witches are in on it too? Not Baba, though. I'm sure Baba's okay."

Avery nodded. "I can't explain the feeling I had when I saw Acton, Low. It was so strong. I *knew* him. It was like we were connected. After all these years of not knowing where I come from or where I really belong, suddenly I felt... *right*. Is that strange? Just looking at him made me feel like I'd come home."

"Seriously Avery, you think *that's* the strange bit of all this?" Low shook his head.

Avery ignored him. "I can't let him go now I've seen him. If there's even the smallest chance that Bean Nighe is right and I can find Acton, I've got to take it."

"I'm not sure I want to go back to any place Mab is in charge. Are you sure we should go to the library?"

"I think it's the safest place, Low. For whatever reason, Mab's not prepared to attack me openly. That will protect us at Cunningfoot."

They fell into silence again. Trudging uphill in the dark, they had no real sense of how far they had walked until Low cried out, "Hey! Can you hear that?"

Noises came out of the gloom, dimly at first, then louder and louder, before they heard the unmistakeable rattle and clang of the railway station. They broke into a run. Gradually they could pick out the hum of human voices, until at last they could see sunlight streaming in from a tunnel entrance.

A high wire fence barred their way into the station, but Avery sprinted up and over. "Give me a sec," puffed Low behind her. "I want to try something." He thrust his arms out at right angles and scrunched his eyes up tight, concentrating so hard his tongue poked out. After a moment's pause, beginning at the tips of his fingers, he transformed into an owl.

With a little run up, he took to the air, alighting safely next to Avery on platform four before turning back into his usual form, albeit with the addition of a pleased grin.

Shouldering their way through the crowds, the pair left the busy station for the library, glad to feel the autumn sunshine on their faces once again.

11

Outside the library a familiar figure in enormous slippers was pacing up and down. Avery and Low saw Baba recognise them amidst the mass of tourists and shoppers. She flapped towards them, her arms outstretched. "Oh, my dears! Where have you been?"

She ushered them hurriedly into the library foyer, casting uneasy looks into the street behind them. Edgar slammed the great door and waved his many hands, muttering protection spells. Inside the library, the human staff and visitors bustled about, oblivious to the little group collected on the doormat.

Cassandra appeared at Avery's elbow, her face full of concern. "You've been gone a long time," she said. "What happened?"

"We went down to Canonmills like you suggested," replied Avery, anxious to fill them in. "We were attacked by the Badoch again! Did you tell anyone where we were going, Cassandra?"

Baba looked aghast. "The Badoch? They attacked you in broad daylight, here in Edinburgh?"

"I… I…" Cassandra's eyes rose nervously to the landing of the grand staircase. "I believe Edgar may have passed on the information."

Watching them from the top of the stairs, one white hand gripping the bannister rail, was Mab. Tall, red-haired and obviously displeased.

Avery was filled with fury. She wanted nothing more than to blurt out everything she knew, but she couldn't risk it. Mab was too dangerous. She might try to do to them what she had done to Acton, and then who would be left to bring him back?

"It is worse than we thought. We must hurry," interrupted Baba. "Fortunately, I have already made the necessary preparations, now we must not delay." She went over to the front desk and collected two thick travelling cloaks, passing one each to Avery and Low.

Edgar tentatively opened the library door again, scanning the street outside for danger. As Cassandra helped Avery with her cloak, Avery took her chance.

"Cassandra," she whispered. "Thank you for what you did today. I know it was risky with the Badoch about and everything, but it was worth it. We saw Bean Nighe. I had a vision of Acton. We know the truth!"

Cassandra's eyes widened and she glanced uneasily up at the bannister, but Mab was no longer there. She was sweeping down the staircase towards them.

Cassandra quickly turned her back on Mab and the others, shielding Avery from view.

"Hurry, take this." She pulled something from the folds of her dress and placed it in Avery's hand. Avery looked down. There lay a delicate gold chain, and from it hung a blue sapphire the colour of harebells.

"What's this? It's beautiful," whispered Avery.

"It's a gift, Avery. I want you to have it. It may be a long time until we see each other again. This will remind you of me," said Cassandra. "Quickly, put it on and tuck it under your clothes. The others will think I'm soppy, so let's keep it a secret, just between you and me."

Avery fastened the chain and smiled up at Cassandra, trying to show her that she understood. Another special object to add to the collection. Maybe this one would help them find Acton.

"Come, Cassandra," called Mab. "I think you have said sufficient farewells."

Cassandra jumped at Mab's voice and hurried out of the way. Avery was sure she was trembling. It was clear Cassandra was terrified of Mab.

Avery scowled as Mab reached out a cold hand and patted Avery stiffly on the shoulder. "May raven's wings guide your travels."

"Time to go, Avery!" a voice boomed from somewhere

above as Glaurt's large hand descended and swung her into the air.

"Wait!" exclaimed Avery. She realised she still didn't know what Cassandra wanted them to do next to find Acton.

"No time, no time," sang Glaurt merrily. As Avery was hoisted upwards, she caught sight of a whiskery black nose poking out from beneath Cassandra's curls. So Low was right, Cassandra did have a pet rat.

The library door was enormous, but Glaurt was still too big to fit through it with ease, so he thrust his hand outside into the street and deposited Avery in a heap on the pavement next to Baba and Low, who had already gone outside.

"Mwah!" The troll blew a big kiss after her then slammed the door shut.

A tandem bicycle was propped against the library wall. On the front was a wicker basket, and a paraffin lamp swung from a metal crook attached to the handlebars. Baba wheeled it over.

"Baba, please, we need to tell you something." Avery scrambled to stand.

"There's no time, Avery dear. You *must* go. There is nothing more important than getting you to safety," replied Baba. There was a slight tremor in her voice.

"Baba, we—"

"On you get!" Baba steadied the bicycle for them.

"Baba—" Avery tried again as she clambered onto the front seat of the tandem, but the witch put her hand up to silence her, glancing hurriedly over her shoulder. "Please trust me, Avery. You're going somewhere very secret and very safe."

"And we're cycling there?" asked Avery.

"It can't be far then," added Low, brightening.

"I'm afraid it is quite far, dear," replied Baba as she helped him onto the rear seat.

Avery shook her head. They couldn't leave now. How would they ever find Acton? Baba misread Avery's vexed expression. "Not to worry, dear. This old gal will get you there. Sparrow here knows the way." Baba patted the handlebars affectionately. "Just start pedalling and the bicycle will do the rest."

"What, no map or directions?" asked Low.

"You don't need them. I've told Sparrow where to take you. It won't deviate," replied Baba.

"Baba, that's not it…" Avery cried, feeling desperate.

Baba fixed Avery with a firm stare. "Avery, something very important is lost. We witches came to the library to look for it, but for some reason we can't remember what it is. Someone is removing all information linked to it." She leaned in close. "We think that's why that book was murdered last night. This is powerful magic, Avery. And in these troubling times, I wonder whether more than just the fate of the magical world may rest on us finding it. It is essential we get you away from here. You must go!"

Avery's brain whirred. A lost thing linked to Whimbrel Baxter's book? Perhaps…

But before she could protest, Baba gave them a surprisingly swift push for a person so small and they were off, picking up speed along the bumpy pavement.

"Wait, Baba… That's just it…" Avery tried to call over her shoulder, but her words were swallowed by the bicycle's pace. She frantically pulled on the brakes, but they didn't seem to work.

"Watch out!" Low warned passers-by.

"Just pedal!" Baba hollered.

Avery braced for a crash as she and Low careered towards a busy intersection. The bicycle creaked and swayed, then the front wheel lifted off the ground with a lurch.

"Stop that, Avery!" shouted Low.

"It's not me!" she yelled back. "It's the bicycle!"

With a pop and a ping, the back wheel lifted off the ground too. No one on the busy street seemed to notice a bicycle flying past their noses with two children clinging on desperately.

Up, up it climbed, until they were far above the city, the wispy edges of clouds tracing patterns on their cheeks.

12

As the bicycle rose high over the rooftops, the city dwindled into a grey haze beneath them.

"Do you think we need to keep pedalling?" asked Low.

"No idea…" Avery replied. "Let's try stopping."

They lifted their feet from the pedals. Almost instantly the front wheel started to dip and they began to lose height.

"I'd say that's a yes!" said Avery. They both cycled furiously until the bicycle was back on course.

"Oh dear," grumbled Low, whose short legs were already beginning to tire. "I don't think Baba realised that we haven't had any lunch."

"Hang on." Avery leaned forward to inspect the wicker basket and pulled out two brown-paper packages. "Sandwiches!" she declared. "And that one smells suspiciously like mouse pâté to me – ugh!"

"Baba's amazing!" Low beamed, managing to unwrap his sandwich one-handed, while he held his handlebar with the other.

As they munched, the cloud grew thicker, and soon they weren't able to see beyond either wheel of the bicycle. The paraffin lamp fired up by itself, illuminating dense banks of rolling grey cloud.

"Oh Low, that was absolute disaster," groaned Avery. "I tried to tell Cassandra about Acton but then Mab appeared. Cassandra's terrified of her! And Baba wouldn't let me get a word in. What if the lost thing Baba and the other witches are looking for wasn't a thing at all? What if it's Acton? Baba said they thought it was something to do with the murdered book – the one with Acton's father's name on it. It can't be a coincidence, can it? And why can't they remember what they're searching for? If they're looking for him at the library, we've got no hope of finding him if we're cycling in the opposite direction." Avery sighed.

"I don't see why would they come to a library to look for a person. You can't keep a person on a shelf like you can a book," said Low. "You know what keeps niggling at me? Bean Nighe called Acton Baxter 'the magic man' and they're the same words used in that prophecy about you.

"*Tale bites tale, pierced heart,*
family bonds and corrupted arts,
Flame-red hair, kindles bad,
rodent-hearted and power-mad,

Memories lost, dark loch,
hidden path 'neath city rock,
Magic man, youth reborn,
preserved awhile by Cat Fae lore,
Hearts bond, hearts weep,
hearts told and histories keep,
Forgotten beast, foot to claw,
airborne, the Great Wyrm's flaw,
Tales stolen, tales remade,
by a tale told, a history's paid.

That's how it goes, isn't it? I memorised it."

Avery almost stopped pedalling. "You're right!"

Low puffed out his chest and adjusted his glasses. "And what about 'hidden path 'neath city rock'? Don't you think that could be the railway tunnel?"

Avery's mind raced. Could it really be that parts of the prophecy were coming true? The sapphire bumped against her chest.

"Oh, I forgot to tell you. Cassandra gave me this beautiful pendant. Can you see?" She tried to turn to show Low the necklace but the bicycle leaned dangerously to one side.

"Show me later!" cried Low as Avery quickly spun back round. "That was nice of her."

"It was, wasn't it? I knew it was Cassandra sending me the objects. I reckon this necklace is going to help us in some way, just like the peach stone and the guidebook. She must have a plan for us to find Acton, even if we are miles away from the library. She told me to keep the sapphire a secret, but I don't think she meant from you."

Low sat up straight. "Er, Avery. Something's happening to your back pocket."

Avery turned around, making Sparrow lean again. Low was right. A bright light was streaming out of the top of her pocket. She reached her hand in and pulled out the piece of sea glass.

A ray of light shot out from it, like the beam of a lighthouse, penetrating the clouds far into the distance. At the same moment, Sparrow's front wheel turned a hard left, flinging Avery and Low to one side.

The bicycle seemed to be following the light from the sea glass. Avery stared down at it in her palm. The frosted texture was gone, the surface now clear and shiny. Engraved on it was an image of the sun.

"Look, Low!" Avery held it up for him to see. "You said you thought there was something underneath."

At that moment Sparrow veered sharply to the right. Avery clung to the handlebars as they returned to their previous course.

Almost immediately, the bicycle swerved *again* and they were back following the beam of light.

"What's going on?" cried Low. "Baba said it knew where it was going!"

Sparrow switched direction once again, then snapped back, tracking the beam.

"I'm going to be sick," he moaned.

"I think the stone is pulling us over this way, but Sparrow's trying to follow Baba's directions," Avery said. The bicycle was now swinging sharply back and forth like a gate in a gale.

"Please," she called out to the bicycle. "I know Baba's given you instructions, but I think Cassandra meant for us to follow this light. I promise we'll get straight on with the journey to Baba's place of safety afterwards."

"What are you saying, Avery?" Low demanded, his knuckles white. "I'm completely fine with not following the light, thank you very much. Baba's place of safety sounds just great to me!"

"What if this sea glass leads us to Acton?" Avery asked. "We need to find him!"

Sparrow's efforts to resist the beam became weaker and weaker until at last it seemed to give in, aligning its front wheel with the direction of the light.

"Thanks, Sparrow." Avery gave the handlebars a grateful pat.

Low sighed loudly behind her. "Personally, I've had

enough surprises to last me a lifetime, but if you insist on choosing the most dangerous path every time, then so be it... I just hope you don't get us killed, Avery Buckle!"

13

They cycled on in silence. Low sulked but Avery ignored him, pushing any doubts out of her mind with each downward thrust of the pedals. She squinted into the distance, trying to catch first sight of wherever it was they might be heading. They had been travelling for hours, and even through the dense cloud she could see that the sun was setting. Gradually, pockets of night sky appeared in the cloud, pricked with the glint of stars. Avery pulled her travelling cloak tighter to shield against the cold evening air.

Her thoughts were interrupted when the beam of light suddenly swung downwards, pointing to the ground. Sparrow shot after it.

"Averrrry!" cried Low from the back of the tandem.

They both only just managed to cling on as the wind rushed up, their hair streaking out behind them. Avery squeezed her eyes shut as they careered towards the ground, the sound of Low's shrieks loud in her ears.

They landed with a painful bump.

The bicycle bounced over rough tussocks of grass before coming to a standstill in front of a pair of enormous iron gates, then bucked, knocking both Avery and Low to the ground. It shook its handlebars and rang its bell with a shrill 'Brrriinngg!' as if offended by its rough treatment.

Avery got to her feet, dusting her knees, but Low lay motionless on the grass.

"Am I dead?" he moaned. "I must be dead."

The wind picked at Avery's hair. Open moorland covered rolling hills, broken by a black outline of woodland not far away. The rise and fall of the landscape cast long shadows beneath the starlit night sky.

Avery gazed at the closed gates in front of them, which hung from a huge metal archway as tall as a house. The archway wasn't attached to anything, no walls or accompanying building. She peered through gaps in the intricately curled ironwork for a park or grand driveway beyond, but there was nothing, just rough grass.

Why would anyone put gates like this in such a remote place? Avery stood back, craning her neck to try and read words welded into the arch:

But as she touched the gates, the letters rearranged themselves and new ones appeared. Avery read them aloud: "'In memory of Acton Baxter, whose betrayal brought destruction on this place.'"

She shivered.

"What did you say?" asked Low, his eyes still closed.

"Low, you're not dead, but someone thinks Acton is. Look, the letters in the arch just changed. 'In memory'– that means someone has died."

Low got slowly to his feet with a dramatic sigh and wheeled the tandem up to the archway, leaning the bicycle against it. He followed Avery's eyeline, reading the words out to himself.

"That's not creepy at all!" he said sarcastically. "What is this place? Some sort of memorial?"

Avery put her hand out and touched the cold ironwork again. The letters jostled then faded until only the first message remained. 'In memory'… the words had seemed so certain. She shook her head.

"What if Bean Nighe is wrong, Low? I want to believe that Acton's alive so much. I want to think he's just lost somewhere and all I need to do is to find him. But I saw it with my own eyes: Mab destroyed him. No one could come back from that."

Low hopped awkwardly from foot to foot, not knowing quite what to say.

Avery wiped her nose with her sleeve. "The awful thing is, I think I'd be sadder for myself than for him if we couldn't find him. Because I don't know him really, do I? Here I am dreaming of finally belonging somewhere, or at least with someone, but maybe Acton isn't the answer."

Low stood close beside her. "Don't give up yet, Avery. Not until we know for certain that there's no hope. Do you want to look around? I mean, the sea glass brought us here, which means Cassandra must have wanted us to come. Maybe there's something here that will help us?"

Avery nodded. "Yeah, alright. Thanks, Low. I know you didn't want to follow the sea glass."

Low took the lantern from the bicycle and held it up as Avery pushed on one of the gates. It swung open with a creak. They both took a sharp intake of breath.

There was something on the other side after all, something that could only be seen by stepping through the open gate.

The ruins of a once grand castle rose up, dark and ominous against the starry sky. Between hollow archways and empty windows Avery could see the flickering shapes of bats. The wind moaned through the vacant, roofless rooms. Over to the left, a derelict cottage slumped to the ground. It must have been some sort of gatehouse. Everything was burnt and blackened as if there had been a great fire. The whole place was ghostly.

Avery took a step forward. Out of the darkness, something hard and round suddenly hit her squarely on the top of her head. "OW!"

Then another.

"OW!"

And another.

"OWWW!"

A voice echoed off the ruins. "Go away or I'll keep throwing – I'm warning you! You need to leave!"

Avery kicked one of the round objects. It was a peach stone. They were being bombarded with peach stones!

"Who's there?" shouted Avery, rubbing her head.

"I am!" replied the voice. "And I'm telling you to go!"

The voice came from high above them. Avery craned her neck to see the top of the arch, where a boy who looked to be about her own age had appeared. Both he and the castle must have been hidden by some kind of invisibility spell.

"Look, we're not here to cause any trouble," she called up to him.

"I don't doubt it," the boy called back. "But you still need to leave. Now!"

He took hold of the archway with both hands, curled up his legs and leapt off.

"Oh my goodness!" cried Low, covering his eyes with his hands.

The boy landed gracefully with a small hop beside Avery. It was a jump and landing that she couldn't have pulled off much better herself.

Up close, Avery thought he looked a lot like a shipwrecked sailor. The sleeves of his stripy T-shirt were torn, and his tattered trousers had been cut off at the calves. To complete the look, his raggedly chopped sandy hair flopped across his face and his bare feet were filthy.

"It's not you causing trouble that I'm worried about," the boy said, rising from his impressive landing. "It's *her*. If *she* comes, we're all in for it!"

14

"Who are you talking about? Who's *she?*" Avery asked. The boy kept glancing nervously up at the night sky. Whoever this person was, he was genuinely scared of her.

The boy shook his head, tossing a peach stone up into the air and catching it again, as if preparing for another throw. "I've told you, get back on your bicycle and go."

"Avery, maybe we should do as he says…" murmured Low, eyeing the peach stone.

But Avery didn't move. There was something intriguing about this boy. About this place. Avery gazed at him. "What are you doing here all on your own in the middle of the night?"

"I'm not on my own." He threw the peach stone to the ground.

Avery and Low exchanged glances. There was certainly no one else around that they could see. Avery turned and walked towards the castle.

"What on earth happened here anyway?"

"Look, you really need to leave," persisted the boy, striding after her. "She could turn up at any moment."

Avery paused in front of one of the blackened ruined walls. The fire here must have been an inferno to cause so much damage. She put her hand out and touched the charred stone.

The light around her changed. Avery found herself blinded by bright sunshine and blue skies. There was warmth on her back, but the acrid smell of burning filled her nostrils.

In the distance she could just hear Low calling: "Avery? Oh, for goodness' sake... Yep, she's gone again!" Then his voice faded and was replaced by someone else's.

"We've let her down badly, Baba." A familiar voice spoke beside her. Avery turned to see Ghilli smack his fist into his palm. Next to him stood Baba, and behind them both smoke rose in spirals from the smouldering ruins of the castle. The fire that had destroyed it had only recently been put out.

Avery looked down at her hand, still feeling the night air and the cold stone of the castle wall beneath her fingers. She had touched the casket in the library and then seen Mab about to destroy it. And her fingers had grazed the walls just before she had the vision of Acton and Mab in the tunnel. Her visions must be activated by touch!

"I don't understand what Avery was doing here anyway," continued Ghilli, his brow furrowed. *"This old castle of the*

Lammermuirs has been abandoned for years now. Why would she come here?"

"We can't know. Perhaps she was looking for clues about what happened to them," Baba replied with a sigh.

"Someone wanted to make Avery's death here look like an accident, but the evidence all points to it being the very opposite. She thought someone was after her in her first life and nobody believed her. She thought someone was after her again in this second life and still nobody believed her. Now she's gone again, we must all see the truth. Someone is hunting her through her nine lives! We have to find out who is doing this, Baba, and you know I have my suspicions."

"You're right, Ghilli, we didn't take her concerns seriously. There's no doubt in my mind now that Avery was murdered both this time and before, but—"

"Mab is the one who's behind it, I'm certain," Ghilli burst out. "Once a Logan, always a Logan!"

Baba shook her head. "Come now, Ghilli, your grief is clouding your judgement. Mab has proved herself beyond any doubt. She isn't like her father."

"I knew it!" Avery muttered to herself. "Mab is the one who's after me. She killed Acton. And she's right there at Cunningfoot!"

"How can you be so blind, Baba?" Ghilli demanded.

Baba shook her head again. "There are more important things at hand now. We need to find where Avery has been *reborn and prepare a place of safety for her. Ceridwen has an idea about using ancient guardian-spell magic to look after Avery until she is of age and can have her history explained to her...*

Ghilli opened his mouth to reply, but Avery didn't hear what he said. As he, Baba and the sunlit skies faded, Avery felt for the ruins, willing the vision to carry on. She ran her fingers blindly across the stonework but nothing happened.

"Is she going to be alright? She doesn't look at all well." The boy's voice broke in. Avery was back amongst the shadowy ruins with a headache blooming behind her eyes. "Maybe you should come and get something to eat. You look a bit grey. And it would be nice to have visitors for once..." He frowned. "Knuckle won't be happy, but I can't just leave you out here if you're not well."

The boy glanced uneasily up at the sky. "You don't want to get caught by *her*. Knuckle says she blasts any living thing in sight with sparks that come out of her finger. Honestly, rabbits, mice, birds... but she especially hates cats. There was this stray up here once and, well..." He shuddered at the thought, his voice trailing away. "I like cats..."

His words made Avery's headache throb harder. She closed her eyes and saw the message on the gates: *'whose betrayal brought destruction on this place'*. Only one person would think that Acton had somehow betrayed them.

"Who's *she?*" Avery asked again, more urgently this time.

"The witch. She comes here sometimes, though lately she's been coming more often. She's the one who burned the castle down. Knuckle nearly died when she set light to the gatehouse. She doesn't know he survived and that he's still here. And she certainly doesn't know about me. Knuckle always makes us hide when she visits, so I've never seen her properly, but I've seen what she can do." He pushed aside a shock of grubby blond hair that had flopped into his eyes and regarded Avery with concern. "Come on, I really think it would be a good idea for you to rest for a while."

The boy turned, beckoning them to follow.

As they hurried after him, Low whispered, "What did you see?"

"I saw Baba and Ghilli talking," Avery whispered back. "I died here in the fire, Low, but it wasn't the first time I'd been killed. I was already on my second life."

Low's eyes widened. "Your second life! She said she'd hunt you through your nine lives. The witch that boy keeps talking about is Mab!"

"It must be," nodded Avery grimly. "It explains why the sea glass brought us here. Cassandra wanted me to learn more about what Mab has been up to. But if that boy's right, Mab might be back at any moment. Every second we spend here I'm in danger. We need to leave, as soon as we can."

They were approaching the derelict gatehouse. The wall at one end was still intact, the chimney poking out from the top of it. Remains of the slate roof slumped down from the wall to the ground, and heaps of blackened stonework and charred wooden beams lay scattered all around. The boy was waiting for them beside a pile of stones heaped up by the fallen roof.

"You'll feel better when you've got some food inside you," he said with a smile. "This way." He ducked in amongst the stones, disappearing from sight through a narrow gap between the rubble.

15

In contrast to the cold night air outside, the space underneath the fallen roof was warm and cosy. The original fireplace filled the end wall and still seemed to work, a fire blazing in its hearth. Slices of bacon spat in a frying pan, and tattie scones crackled on a griddle. Avery's stomach rumbled at the delicious smell. She suddenly realised how hungry she was.

A three-legged stool was pulled up at a rickety wooden table, on which stood a storm lantern. Bundles of woollen blankets and bedding were piled up in the corner, and a rocking chair sat by the hearth. In it, a crouched figure prodded the cooking bacon with a wooden spatula. "You've been an age with that firewood, Tab," the figure grumbled.

"Sorry, Knuckle, I got distracted…"

The creature named Knuckle turned and then jumped with alarm, waving the spatula at Avery and Low with a fist that was easily the size of the chipped teapot waiting to be filled by the fire. "What on earth have you dragged

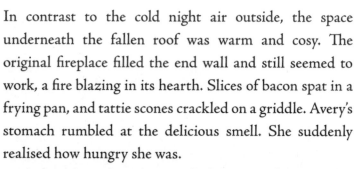

in here?" he cried, glowering through thick lenses set in a pair of enormous black-rimmed spectacles.

"Please, Knuckle, I tried to get them to leave but they just need a rest and something to eat," the boy pleaded with a persuasive smile. "There's no harm in that, is there? And we never get visitors... Oh, and sorry, I dropped all the firewood when I saw them arrive – on a flying bicycle, no less!"

"And they were alone?" Knuckle demanded.

"As an elephant in an elevator."

Low muffled a laugh at the joke. Knuckle glared at him.

"Well, I suppose that's one thing to be grateful for," he said, taking in Avery's worried expression. "Fine, you can stay – just for a hot meal, mind." He tutted loudly. "I don't know, parents these days, letting children wander around the countryside in the dead of night!" Knuckle shook the spatula at Avery and Low. "Inadequate levels of supervision, that's what I say."

"Knuckle likes to think he's an expert on parenting," grinned Tab, slinging his arm across Knuckle's broad shoulders. He was so short that the boy could reach easily.

"I've had to be, bringing you up!" Knuckle raised his eyebrows at Tab, but the look he gave the boy was full of tenderness.

"I'm an orphan," Tab explained. "Knuckle here took me in when I was a baby."

Avery found herself trying not to stare. Knuckle was such a strange-looking creature. Tiny black freckles clustered along his hairline and along the backs of his muscular white arms, disappearing underneath his tattered vest.

Frowning at Avery and Low, Knuckle took an enormous orange handkerchief from the pocket of his pinstripe trousers and sneezed into it. A puff of black powder flew up into the air, crinkling into glowing sparks, which died away.

"A flying bicycle, you said? Fancy." He sniffed and shoved his handkerchief back in his pocket. "And do you have names?"

"I'm Avery Buckle and this is Low Hoskings," said Avery.

"Well, Avery Buckle, you've been very lucky. If *she* had been here when you arrived, you'd have been in real trouble. Don't know how she gets here, but it's quick. And you never can tell when she might show up, strutting about like she owns the place."

Knuckle turned and unhooked a blackened kettle from where it hung over the fire. He poured steaming-hot water into the teapot.

"Who is this *she* you're so scared of?" Avery asked.

"I'm not scared! Just have to be careful, that's all. Someone needs to be around to look after the boy," huffed

Knuckle, stirring the pot with a bent spoon. "Anyway, don't know her name. Don't want to. Tall, red hair, sour face."

Avery gave Low a meaningful look.

Knuckle glanced up at Tab. "Off you go and get that firewood you were supposed to bring back. We'll need it tonight."

"Back in a jiffy." The boy hopped up and out through the narrow gap in the rubble with practised ease.

As soon as he was gone, Knuckle continued. "Don't like talking about it too much in front of the boy, but she's a nasty specimen. Years ago she came – furious, full of hate – and destroyed the empty castle. The family weren't here at the time."

Avery frowned. Knuckle can't have known that she had been in the castle at the time of the fire.

"Set fire to it with spell after spell. This gatehouse came down too. Muttering away as she was doing it, she was. You should have heard her, on and on about some poor young chap she'd killed. She thought she'd got rid of me in the fire so she was on her own, but no one decides when Hearth-folk leave a home except Hearth-folk."

"Hearth-folk?" asked Low.

"Hearth-folk keep the home fires burning, so to speak. We look after the house. Not every house has one, of course, but I belong to this house. That's how this old chimney survived no matter what curses *she* sent its way.

That witch might know powerful magic, but she doesn't know the power of a home that's been full of love and laughter." Knuckle looked wistful. "One day the family will come back and I'll have the castle and the gatehouse ready for them. Slowly, slowly I put the old stones back, just one at a time so she doesn't notice."

He lowered his voice. "Kept talking about the Beatha Skelpit spell, she did. That's some of the darkest magic around. Don't think there's a creature in all the magical realms who doesn't know that. Doesn't just kill a person, it turns back the clock until pouf! They're gone! Erased from history and memory. Course, that bit's not instant. To get rid of someone entirely you have to destroy every mention of them in books and letters and what not." He sloshed milk from a jug into four tin beakers.

"So that's what kind of spell it was!" whispered Avery to Low. "She killed him with the Beatha Skelpit spell."

"But why hide the castle like she has? Why not just destroy it so completely that no one would ever know it existed?" Low whispered back.

"There must be some reason, but don't ask me what it is." Avery shrugged wearily. "The point is she thinks she was betrayed. Perhaps she wanted to keep this place so only she would remember what had happened. She must have come back afterwards and cast the invisibility spell."

"Will you two stop muttering and get this tea down you." Knuckle tipped up the pot and poured out the steaming liquid. "Hope you like tattie scones."

"We've got to leave, Mr Knuckle," said Avery. The thought of Mab arriving and ticking off another one of Avery's lives made her feel faint. "We should never have come. We were on our way somewhere else. We only came here because a light appeared out of this." She held out the sea glass. It had frosted over again, the engraving lost to view. "We followed it, but now we need to get back on our journey."

Knuckle sniffed and slapped the scones onto tin plates, ignoring the panic in her voice. "That's a sun stone, that is. They used it to navigate across the seas, long, long ago. Nifty bit of kit and mighty rare." He nudged the bacon out of the frying pan too.

"It's beautiful. Can I see?" asked Tab as he returned, dumping an armful of firewood down by the hearth. Avery passed the glass to him. "Huh, it tingles in my hand!"

Knuckle eyed the boy and then peered intently at the stone. "Hmm, that stone's got a hefty bit of enchantment on it, that's for sure."

That made sense, Avery thought. Cassandra must have cast a spell on it to make it show them the way here – that way they would learn more about Mab's plot.

"Now, once you two have had some nourishment, you'll need to be on your way," said Knuckle, pushing their plates towards them.

"What?" Tab looked shocked. "Knuckle, they can't go anywhere now. It's dangerous out there. What if they bump into *her* as they're flying away? Can't they stay here tonight and go in the morning?"

Knuckle scowled at the boy, before finally heaving a long-suffering sigh. "Alright." He turned to Avery and Low. "But you go at first light, you hear me?"

Tab put his hand in Knuckle's mighty palm and smiled at him. The affection between them was plain to see. It gave Avery a sense of hope. Knuckle was right. Despite the absence of four standing walls, the cosy little gatehouse did feel like a home, and she was glad this funny, caring boy had someone to look after him.

Low wolfed down his scones as if he had never eaten in his life. It turned out near-death experiences on flying bicycles worked up quite an appetite. Avery sipped on her tea and felt herself relax. As they ate, Knuckle told stories about the mischief Tab had got into when he was little, like the time he'd gorged himself on a whole batch of Knuckle's homemade sweet Scottish tablet and been violently sick. Tab, grinning, protested and teased him back. The fire burned low before Knuckle said with a sigh, "Enough blethering, now. It's time for bed."

Tab groaned.

"Come on, Avery and Tab, you clear the dishes. Low, you can help me." Knuckle began arranging the piles of bedding on the floor.

"Do you know any good jokes?" Tab asked, reluctantly stacking the mugs. "Knuckle's aren't funny. And I've heard them all a million times before." Avery smiled to herself. She would say the same thing about Bob. It struck her how alike she and Tab were.

"Jokes?" she replied. "Actually I do. What's a cat's favourite colour?"

As Avery regaled Tab with some of Bob's best worst jokes, she realised just how much she missed her guardian spells. Cindy would have had Tab scrubbed, hair cut and suitably clothed in no time.

"You know I'm an orphan too," said Avery.

"Are you?" Tab seemed surprised.

"Yeah, there are these two people who look after me. They're called Bob and Cindy. They're wonderful, mostly, but… sometimes I feel like I don't quite belong. Like I haven't… found my true home yet. Does that make sense?"

Tab nodded. "It's nice to know I'm not the only one who isn't quite sure where they fit," he said quietly.

When the dishes were done and the beds were ready, Knuckle damped down the fire and they snuggled under their blankets.

In the flickering lantern light, Avery looked up and considered the gnarly old beams that supported what remained of the roof. It must have been a beautiful gatehouse at one time.

"What did this place used to be like, Knuckle?" she asked.

"Well, now, let me see," he said, propping his head up with his huge hand. "A long, long time ago, the castle and this gatehouse were built by a great family. The Lammermuirs, they were called. One of the seven clans of Scotland charged with keeping balance in the magical world, and proud of it."

The Lammermuirs? Of course, their name had been above the gate. Avery remembered Bean Nighe had mentioned them in one of her riddles too. She looked over to Low, but his eyelids were already drooping.

Knuckle continued. "They used to come in the summer every year and spend the warm months up here in the hills. All the family, and their friends too. There were games and feasting and magic, and so much laughter. I was young Hearth-folk then." He looked wistfully around him at the crumbling building. "There was another wall at the end, in those days. The front door was over there."

Knuckle gestured with his great hands, seeing the old house rising up from his memories.

Avery followed his movements with her eyes, the walls rebuilding themselves in her mind. It felt so real she could almost feel the sunshine pouring in through the windows.

"Part of the roof was glass," he went on. "A great peach tree grew up inside it, and the ceiling was covered in its leaves. And those peaches! My mouth waters just thinking on it. Never tasted anything like them before or since. Long gone, of course. The odd peach stone is all that's left now."

He smiled sadly and looked over at Tab and Low. They were fast asleep, their breathing slow and steady. Knuckle turned out the lantern.

"She hasn't won," Avery whispered into the darkness. "She thinks she has, but she hasn't."

"Who's that?"

"The witch... the one who destroyed this place."

"Hmpf," said Knuckle softly. "You try telling *her* that."

16

Avery was woken by a chink of sunlight shining onto her face from a crack in the tumbledown wall of the gatehouse. A low fire in the hearth hissed and crackled, but otherwise she was alone. The blankets nearby had been thrown back carelessly.

She sat up and rubbed her eyes. Where was Low? They needed to go before Mab showed up, so they could reach Baba's place of safety. Then they could work out how to find Acton.

Laughter and voices drifted in, so Avery pulled herself to the edge of the bedding and put on her shoes.

Outside, the morning was bright and fresh. In daylight, the burnt-out castle looked even eerier than it had in darkness.

"You're awake then." Knuckle sat on a wooden plank balanced between two piles of stones, taking satisfied gulps from a giant tin mug of coffee. Beside him were a blackened cooking pot and some licked-clean bowls.

"Where's Low? We need to go," said Avery, sounding grumpier than she meant to.

Knuckle pointed to a water pump not far away. Tab was leaning on its long arm, and he and Low were both laughing. Water spurted out, drenching Low as he tried to wash his face.

"Sit down, Avery. There's porridge in the pot. They've had theirs already."

"We need to *go*," persisted Avery.

"You said that," replied Knuckle. "Won't get far on an empty stomach though. Besides, it's still early."

Avery gave in and sat down. As she lifted the lid off the pot, the delicious smell made her stomach rumble. Maybe breakfast was a good idea after all.

"How long had the castle been empty before it was burned down, Knuckle?" she asked between mouthfuls.

"Oh, not that long," he replied. "She would never have got away with it if the family had been here."

Avery looked at him. "What happened to them?"

He stared back at her from behind his thick lenses. "I don't know. I'm Hearth-folk so I can't leave my hearth to go and find out. All I can think is that it was something bad. Magic is thinning in Scotland – you can feel it missing from the air. And that means all sorts of wicked things can happen. There was a time long ago when the magic in Scotland was this thin. These hills we're standing on hadn't even been born then. That was a terrible time. The time of the Crannogs."

Avery's spoon stopped halfway to her mouth. Her mind shot back to the monster sleeping under Edinburgh.

"The Crannogs?" repeated Low. He and Tab had returned from the pump without being noticed.

But Knuckle was already swinging himself down off the bench. "It's time you were off. It's bad luck to talk of these things."

"Please, Knuckle," begged Avery. "What do you know about the Crannogs?"

"Be on your way now. I've got jobs to do. Safe travels to you." Knuckle nodded and then strode away, taking the empty breakfast bowls with him.

"What were you talking about? Whatever it was, it's upset him," said Tab, glancing after Knuckle with a frown. He sighed. "I wish you didn't have to go. But I suppose you had better. It's not safe to stay. It's magic how fast *she* arrives. She must be a powerful witch."

They gathered up their belongings and followed Tab, who guided them through the ruins and back out of the gates. Sparrow the bicycle stood upright outside the arch, and it rang its bell when it saw them, obviously eager to be off.

Avery and Low clambered aboard.

Avery felt strangely sad. In spite of the danger they were in, she found herself not wanting to say goodbye. It had been fun and, even if only briefly, she had forgotten about her worries.

"It's been nice having visitors," Tab said quietly. He looked as forlorn as Avery felt. "You know, it really is a great bicycle," he continued, stroking Sparrow's handlebars. The bike tilted towards him slightly. "Maybe, you might come again one day and I could have a ride?"

Impulsively Avery leaned across and gave him a tight hug, whispering, "I hope you find somewhere you fit, Tab." She sat back. "We'd love to come and see you again, wouldn't we, Low?"

"Of course," he replied. "As long as Knuckle has some of those tattie scones on the go."

Tab broke into a wide smile that lit up his face. "Until then..."

"Until then," repeated Avery with a nod.

She and Low pushed down on the pedals of the bicycle and away from the gates. The moorland grass was horrible to ride over but they eventually got up some speed and the front wheel lifted. Then they were airborne, waving down at Tab outside the gates, until he was nothing but a tiny stitch in the blanket of green below.

Up in the clouds they pedalled on and on, Sparrow's chain squeaking with each turn of the wheels. Avery kept a wary eye out for any sign of Mab, but her thoughts kept turning to Acton. The need to find him beat like a drum in her heart. "I hate this cloud," she grumbled. "It feels like we're not going anywhere."

"It's always like that when you want to get somewhere quickly," replied Low sagely.

Avery sighed heavily then looked down at her hands in surprise. The bicycle handlebars were quivering beneath her palms. She frowned. "Hey, what's wrong with Sparrow?"

Suddenly the tandem shot off course. It zigzagged from side to side as if uncertain which way was best. Avery and Low hung on, their hair flattened to their scalps.

"Not again!" yelled Low.

"No, this is different. It feels like it's afraid of something," Avery shouted back. "Which probably means…"

"… that we should be afraid too!" Low finished, as they broke out of the cloud into clear blue skies. "Hey, what's that?" he yelled. Something was moving towards them at great speed, swimming through the air like an eel in a river.

As it emerged into the clear sky, they saw giant wings, a spiky tail and trailing tendrils sprouting from an angular, scaly head.

Low gulped, then screamed: "D-D-DRAGON!"

The bicycle shuddered and shook as it whizzed through the air. Avery and Low could barely match the movements of their legs with the spinning pedals. On and on Sparrow hurtled, desperate to shake off the monstrous creature pursuing them.

"We can't beat it!" shrieked Low. "A dragon is much, much faster than a bicycle!"

PING! WHOOSH!

An arrow shot past Low's left ear from below, followed by a shout.

"The dragon has them in its sight! We must head it off!" The voice was gruff and fierce.

A volley of arrows followed the first, bouncing off the dragon as a jet of blue flames rocketed from its mouth.

"I didn't think I'd be seeing you two again so soon," came a familiar voice. "And being chased by a bewitched dragon to boot!"

"Ghilli!" Avery and Low turned to see him drawing up beside them on the back of his handsome faery stallion, Kest.

"Come on! My friend Wulver and some of the other faery folk are going to try to hold it back while Kest and I get you down to Inchmahome." Ghilli tied a strong cord to Sparrow's handlebars. "Hang on, it's going to get a bit wild!"

The sky was thick with arrows but the dragon's gnarled scales were like armour, and the missiles caused only annoyance rather than injury. The beast scorched the sky with burning flames, sending the faery folk reeling away.

Ghilli and Kest dived downwards, galloping through the air as if they were thundering along a racecourse.

There was a brief moment when the bicycle hung suspended in the sky, Avery and Low clinging, white-knuckled, to the handles.

"It's going to catch us!" cried Low, but then the rope pulled taut and they were dragged in Kest's wake, spiralling towards earth.

17

The dragon had spotted their change of course. With a roar, it pointed its ugly snout downwards and sent itself into free fall. Shouts went out among the faery folk and a hail of arrows followed it.

On the bicycle, Avery and Low sped along behind Kest, the dragon hot on their heels. The updraft roared in their ears. Barely able to see, they could just make out purple mountains circling an expanse of sparkling water below.

"We're going to drown!" yelped Low, as they plummeted towards the shimmering surface. He and Avery shut their eyes tight, but Kest pulled upwards just in time. Sparrow swung round behind him, skimming the loch.

Avery looked up. Maybe only a hundred metres above, the dragon had stopped. Its red eyes blazed and its spiked tail flicked angrily as it watched them. The beast gave a snarl of fury and then flew off into the clouds.

"We made it!" shouted Ghilli, fist in the air. "Even that fiend didn't dare breach the magical defences of Inchmahome."

Behind them, riders cheered. Ghilli towed the bicycle towards a cluster of wooded islands, bringing it alongside a jetty. Avery could hear music and singing in the distance as Ghilli leapt nimbly onto the dock. Low attempted some nimble leaping of his own but didn't quite carry it off.

"That was amazing! That dragon had no chance of catching us." He puffed out his chest and tried to copy Ghilli's stance.

"Not quite what you were saying when we were up there." Avery slowly peeled her stiff fingers away from Sparrow's handlebars and climbed onto the jetty. "Is that the bewitched dragon you told the witches about at the library, Ghilli?"

"It's an ollipheist," answered the gruff voice from earlier. "You can tell by the band of brass around its neck. Someone has it under a spell. They don't usually come inland like this, but that one has been harassing our borders for months now."

The owner of the gruff voice came up behind Ghilli with the other faery riders. Low and Avery couldn't help but gape. He was the hairiest creature they'd ever seen. His face was long and thin with sharp teeth and pointed ears, while loping arms reached to his knees, ending in spade-like hands. He sat back on his haunches and a thick bushy tail tapped the jetty.

"This is Wulver," introduced Ghilli. "He's a werewolf, in case you're wondering. Wulver, this is Avery and Low."

"Good morning, Avery, Low." Wulver bowed deeply at them both. "The pleasure is all mine."

"He's such a gent," grinned Ghilli, slapping Wulver on the back.

"It's fortunate we'd stepped up our patrols since the Badoch attacks and happened to chance upon you," said Wulver.

Avery shuddered. She didn't like to think what would have happened if Ghilli and Wulver hadn't been there at just the right moment.

"But what are you doing here, Avery?" asked Ghilli. "Why aren't you at the library?"

"We were attacked by the Badoch so Baba sent us away." Avery shook her head at the memory of the dark shadowy mass chasing her and Low in the park. It seemed like a lifetime ago now. "We were supposed to be getting away to a safe place, but—"

"The Badoch attacked you in Edinburgh? Right under the witches' noses?" Wulver interrupted urgently. He and Ghilli exchanged alarmed glances.

"Well, you're safe here with us at Inchmahome," said Ghilli, quickly changing the subject. "And I've got just the thing to take your mind off it: dinner! You've arrived in perfect time for the Autumn Feast."

Avery gave him a worried smile. As fun as an Autumn Feast sounded, she and Low needed to get to Baba's safe place and start working out how to find Acton. They were wasting precious time.

"You heard Ghilli, Avery," said Low, spotting her expression. "We're safe here. Inchmahome must be the place Baba intended us to come."

Avery shook her head. "That doesn't make any sense. Baba would just have sent us off with Ghilli when he left the library. No, Low, that dragon chased poor Sparrow off course."

But Low wasn't going to be put off. "Well, we can't leave while it's still hanging around, and besides… I'm hungry."

"Well…" Avery didn't know what to say. Low looked so hopeful.

"Excellent! I'll take that as a yes." Ghilli beamed. "Follow me."

They walked up the jetty and were soon completely surrounded by a wood. The last of the season's leaves clung to bare branches, shimmering copper and gold in the autumn sunlight. Huge balls woven from twigs and reeds were strung from the trees. Each had a brightly coloured door and curtained window, with rope ladders and bridges creating pathways between them.

Avery lifted her nose and sniffed the air. It was heavy with spices and the smells of cooking. Long wooden tables had been laid out, sagging under the weight of a great feast. Low's eyes were like saucers.

Everywhere faery folk thronged, laughing and chatting. A band of musicians played a wild and chaotic tune on bizarrely coiled brass instruments that had Avery's toe tapping, however reluctantly. A group of faeries wearing costumes covered in bells danced an intricate jig, while others standing around them clapped out the rhythm.

Ghilli and the other returning riders were greeted with hugs and cheers, while Avery and Low were plied with wooden platters laden with spiced breads, fruit, nuts and sugared cakes.

It all tasted delicious. But the best thing to Avery's eyes was that everyone in Inchmahome had tails. They were all sorts of colours and variations, some striped, some spotted. Here, people didn't hide their tails. Here, having a tail was normal. Maybe, once she had found Acton, and Mab was out of the way, they could come and live at Inchmahome. No need to hide her tail here. If a Cat Fae and her wizard could be happy anywhere, surely it would be in a magical place like this.

Avery's eye was drawn to an assembly of tall, serious-looking faeries who clustered on wooden benches around a central firepit, deep in conversation. They wore beads and bells woven through their hair, and long necklaces and earrings that tinkled when they moved.

"Those are the faery Elders," explained Ghilli, following her line of sight. "They're the leaders of us faery folk. They were the ones who sent me to speak to Mab."

Avery nodded, remembering Ghilli's entrance at the library and the tense conversation that had followed.

"They look like they're talking about something important."

Ghilli nodded. "Even on a feast day, the Badoch attacks and that dragon occupy their minds. The Elders believe that the magical clans have failed us, and fear that soon magic will be so thin there may be no place at all for faeries in this world."

Avery turned towards the sound of happy cries and shouts, where a crowd of small faery children had gathered around Low, pulling on his arms. "Ghilli says you're a Hoolet and that you can fly. Show us! Please!"

Low looked at Avery in confusion.

She shrugged and laughed. "Looks like you're famous."

"Sorry." Ghilli winced. "They love to hear stories about the city when I visit and I didn't think you'd be coming here any time soon."

Avery nudged Low. "Well go on then. Show them what you can do."

Blushing slightly, Low drew a deep breath and adjusted his glasses. His face took on a look of intense concentration until his wings appeared. They wouldn't unfurl properly at first, and he rolled his eyes at Avery, giving the wings a shake.

"I thought I was getting better at this owl thing, but—" He sighed and gave them another shake, which seemed to do the trick.

"Show us how you fly!" clamoured the children.

Low puffed out his chest. He seemed to be warming to the attention. Transforming fully into an owl, he shot into the air.

There was a gasp from the faeries. "A Hoolet! A Hoolet!" they called to each other in wonder.

The next thing Avery knew there was a sickening crack and Low, now fully a boy again, came plummeting back to earth. Not looking where he was going, he had flown into a tree branch and knocked himself out cold. He landed with a smack on the ground.

"Low!" cried Avery, pushing people aside to get to him. "Is he alright?" She knelt down at her friend's side. "He hasn't got the hang of it properly yet. Being an owl that is," she explained, desperately scanning him for injuries.

"I'm alright," protested Low feebly, his freckles standing out more than usual against the pallor of his skin.

"We need to get him to the Haven," said Ghilli with concern, attempting to comfort two of the faery children who had burst into tears.

"Allow me," said Wulver, stooping to gather Low gently in his arms.

18

The Haven was a huge woven ball nestled in a spreading oak tree, set a little away from the others. Wind chimes hung from the branches around it, clinking gently in the breeze. Inside, hammocks were slung from thick beams at intervals across the one large room. In each hammock was a sick or ailing faery. Glass jars full of medicines, syrups and tinctures jostled each other for room on rows of shelves, and herbs hung from the ceiling, scenting the air as Wulver brushed past them with his shaggy head. He lay Low down in one of the hammocks and faery folk scurried around, gently pushing Avery aside to draw a heavily embroidered curtain.

"Please, take a seat," said Wulver, indicating a wooden bench in the middle of the open space. "I'm going to get you some sweet tea. It's the best thing for a shock. Will you be okay if I leave you for a moment to fetch it?"

Avery nodded. She didn't think Low's injury was serious but she still felt a bit shaken up.

"Hello." An elderly faery eased himself down next to her, laying a gnarled walking stick across his knees as Wulver vanished out of sight.

Avery looked up. "Hello," she replied quietly, wishing he would leave her alone with her thoughts.

"That your tail, is it?" asked the old faery. He had sandy coloured skin, creased with wrinkles, and his wiry hair was peppered with grey. A pair of deep-brown eyes peered at Avery with interest. "Never seen a Cat Fae one up close."

Avery blushed, quickly tucking her tail up under her again out of habit. It must have come loose in the panic.

"Hey now, you shouldn't ever be ashamed of your tail. If I still had mine I'd be showing it off, and don't you doubt it. Not many faeries live on after their tail has been cut off, but they think I'm going to be fine. Tutt Pugh's my name."

"Are you one of the faeries who were attacked by the Badoch?" Avery asked, smoothing her tail out again with her hand.

"Oh, you've heard, have you?" replied the old faery.

"I'm Avery Buckle." They shook hands. "I can't imagine life without my tail," she said, then reddened. "Sorry, that wasn't a very thoughtful thing to say."

"It's alright," replied Tutt. "I'm getting used to it.

The pity is, I can't remember all of my tale."

"What do you mean?" asked Avery, confused.

"I mean, I can remember the gist of it but the details are slipping out of my memory. And that's the saddest thing, because I was an excellent storyteller, even if I do say so myself. Although perhaps a little long-winded."

Avery's brow furrowed. "Wait a minute. Do you mean that the tail attached to your body wasn't just an ordinary tail like mine?"

"Here we go." Wulver returned, a mug of steaming tea in his hand. "Good afternoon, sir." He greeted the old faery with a bow.

Tutt nodded. "Wulver, I was just telling this young gal about faery tales."

"Well of course I've heard of faery tales," protested Avery. "I just didn't realise that faeries kept their tales in their tails. Like I didn't know books could be killed. Wait a minute…"

A connection had sparked in her mind. Could it be that this faery's tale and Whimbrel Baxter's murdered book were part of the same puzzle? What had Knuckle said about the Beatha Skelpit spell? Once the spell was cast, the victim was erased from history and memory. But to get rid of someone entirely, every mention of them in books and letters had to be destroyed too. And if in books and letters, then surely also in faeries' tales? Might the murdered book and Tutt's tale have contained information about Acton? Avery's thoughts raced around her brain like hares on a circuit.

Tutt went on. "It's my tale that's keeping me alive, even though my furry tail has gone. Mine was about a magic man who couldn't die because his life was linked to that of another. It's my belief that because he can't die and my tale is about him, I didn't die when my tail was cut off."

Avery's heart pounded. A magic man who couldn't die? It couldn't be a coincidence. Tutt Pugh's tale *must* have been about Acton.

"There were more faeries who were attacked, weren't there?" she asked him urgently. "Did any of them live? Where are they now?"

"Of course!" replied Tutt. "Some were injured much worse than others, but they all survived."

He gestured with his stick to the hammocks hanging from the Haven ceiling. A dozen or so faces peered curiously at Avery from over the edges of the swinging beds.

Avery turned to Tutt, her eyes alight. "And did all their tales have something to do with the magic man?"

Tutt nodded.

"What's going on, Avery?" Wulver asked, looking mystified.

"Hang on, Wulver, sorry. I'll explain later." She couldn't

miss this opportunity to find out more. She turned to the faeries. "Please, can any of you tell me what you remember of your tales?"

"Well, mine has a dastardly villain named Crux Logan." A faery with only a few wisps of hair on her head and no teeth leaned forward eagerly, gripping the edge of her hammock with golden-brown hands. "There was a terrible magical duel between him and another wizard called Whimbrel. Whimbrel beat Crux, and the fiend died, cursing Whimbrel as he did, but Crux's daughter swore to take up his cause."

Avery stared at the old woman. Her tale matched exactly what Mab and Acton had talked about in the tunnel.

"Yes, yes, mine's got that Whimbrel chap in too!" cried another faery, nearly falling out of his hammock in his excitement. "The Baxters and the Cat Fae have been allied for as long as anyone can remember. That Whimbrel and his Cat Fae, they have a casket. A big old wooden thing with leather straps. They put their memories from each life in it."

Avery swallowed hard. Cat Fae? A curse? A casket full of memories? She forced herself to think. In her vision in the train tunnel, Mab had wanted Acton to betray his father's secret way to wake the Crannog. Acton didn't tell, so if the casket contained his father's memories, maybe Mab had tried to find out for herself. Had Mab broken open the casket in the library to get hold of Whimbrel's knowledge? Avery's heart was pounding so hard she could feel it in her ears.

"Well, I don't see how I fit in then," said a faery with a bruised eye, cradling one arm in a sling. "Mine's not about any of them. My tale's about old Magnus Currach. He found that prophecy about the last of the Cat Fae." The faery thrust her nose into Avery's face. "Do you know it? The one that starts 'Tale bites tale, pierced heart...'"

Avery nodded numbly. Of course she knew it. There was a sick feeling rising in her stomach. The prophecy. Her very own prophecy.

Another faery pulled on the singed ends of his grey, looped moustache as he spoke. "The prophecy was where that Whimbrel went wrong. It wasn't Whimbrel who Crux Logan cursed. It was his son! That was a much darker revenge as far as Crux was concerned. That's what my tale's all about. Crux knew Whimbrel's young lad was his life's joy. It's the *boy* who's the magic man in the prophecy. He had his own Cat Fae. In my tale, when Whimbrel heard the prophecy and realised his mistake, they got the young lad's own Cat Fae to share her nine lives with him."

It was too much to take in. Avery could barely make sense of it. *She* was Acton's Cat Fae, so did that mean she had somehow shared her lives with Acton? Hearing of the Cat Fae lives conjured up her vision at the Lammermuirs' castle. Ghilli had said that Avery was already on her second life. He had known all about Mab and the Logans. She needed to speak to him. He would be able to tell her whether there was any truth in these tales.

"What's going on, Avery?" asked Wulver. "What is all this about magic clans and sharing lives?"

Avery shook her head. "I don't know myself, Wulver. Where's Ghilli?"

"He stayed behind to comfort the children, but he's waiting outside now."

Avery stood up and looked to the injured faeries. "Thank you, everyone. I hope you get better soon." Then she turned to Tutt. "Thank you, sir."

"My pleasure, Avery Buckle." Tutt nodded. "And mind what I said about your tail, now."

Avery smiled and let her tail curl out behind her as she waved him goodbye.

19

Ghilli came to meet them as Avery and Wulver climbed down from the Haven. "They told me Low is going to be okay."

"Yeah, he'll be fine. He was just showing off." Avery shook her head impatiently.

"One of the children found these on the floor." Ghilli handed Avery Low's glasses, which were thankfully none the worse for the accident.

"Thanks. Listen, Ghilli, I need to ask you about my past. I've been having visions."

Ghilli looked taken aback by the abrupt change of subject but Avery persisted. "You know I told you that Baba sent us from the library to a safe place? Well, this pulled us off course." She held out the sun stone. "It took us to the Lammermuirs' old castle out in the middle of nowhere. I touched the ruins and I had another vision. I saw you talking to Baba. You were angry that I had died and you wanted to protect me from Mab in my next life. You didn't trust her at all."

Ghilli gaped.

"Yes, exactly," said Avery resolutely. "So I know that you know all about it. I've been reborn and you've known me before, in my past lives. Just how old am I? And how old are you? More to the point, why didn't you say any of this when we saw you before?"

Ghilli sighed. "Yes, okay, Avery, I have known you in your previous lives. Faeries don't age in the same way as other creatures. We age in circles, not straight lines, if that makes sense... You and I have always been good friends. I couldn't say anything at the library because I didn't know how much you knew."

"How much I knew? Okay then, this is what I know," Avery barrelled on. "Before Low and I were attacked by the Badoch, Bean Nighe told me that I'm a wizard's cat. Then in my vision I saw him, my wizard. His name is Acton Baxter and he was arguing with Mab. She killed him with the Beatha Skelpit spell. There's a hideous creature called a Crannog asleep under Edinburgh and Mab wants to raise it and rule the world. Acton was trying to stop her—"

"Wait, wait, wait. There's a Crannog under Edinburgh?" interrupted Ghilli, looking bewildered, but Avery ignored him.

"Acton's not dead. He's alive somewhere. Somehow I've shared my nine lives with him. I'm keeping him alive and

I've got to find him! I'm certain he's the magic man in the prophecy about the Cat Fae. These attacks on the faeries are part of it too. I've just met the faeries who survived the Badoch attacks and every single one of their tales is connected."

"Stop, Avery! Yes, you're right, I don't like or trust Mab. Yes, we have all been trying to protect you, but from what and why, I can't tell you. I..." Ghilli paused, brow furrowed. "I can't seem to... I mean, I just can't remember."

Avery shook her head in disbelief. "I saw you talking to Baba about me in the vision. I suppose you're going to say you've never heard the name Acton Baxter?"

Ghilli sighed, rubbing his forehead.

"Ghilli, think!" she pleaded.

"Honestly, Avery, I don't recognise the name. I mean, maybe there's something..." His voice trailed away.

"Yes?" she asked eagerly.

"No, I-I... I can't explain it. I'm sorry," he replied with a helpless shrug.

Avery considered him, frowning. "Alright. I believe you." She dug the toe of her boot into the soil. Acton had been wiped from history and memory by the Beatha Skelpit spell, so of course no one could remember him. Including Ghilli. It was as if Acton had never existed. And that must be why Baba and the others couldn't remember what they were searching for at the library. Whatever it was, it must be something to do with Acton!

But if no one could remember Acton, that meant no one could help her find out where he might be. Well, if Avery couldn't depend on anyone else for information, she would have to depend on herself. Perhaps her visions might help her to discover more clues?

"I need to see more of these visions, Ghilli. I know they're triggered by touch but that's all. Could I see into the past in my other lives? Can you tell me how to do it?" she asked.

Ghilli shook his head. "Sorry Avery, I-I-I don't know. Maybe you had visions… I just don't remember."

"Can you think of anyone else who might be able to help me?"

Ghilli and Wulver exchanged blank looks.

"That's it then. I'm out of ideas," said Avery glumly. She sighed heavily, but as she breathed in again, the air caught in her throat. She swallowed, but still couldn't take in any air. Her throat was getting tighter and tighter. She couldn't breathe!

Reaching under her clothes, Avery brought out the necklace Cassandra had given her. It had suddenly become unbearably heavy, like a boulder around her neck. Her vision blurred. She buckled, struggling to stay upright.

"Avery! Take it off!" shouted Ghilli.

Avery shook her head mutely, unable to speak. Ghilli looked at Wulver with alarm. "It's killing her! We need to get it off her!"

Avery scrabbled at her neck, fighting for every breath. She crumpled heavily to the floor, and then her world went dark.

Avery woke to the pungent smell of dried herbs and guessed she was lying in a hammock at the Haven. Ghilli and Wulver must have brought her here when she collapsed.

She opened her eyes to see them both warily inspecting something bundled in a dark cloth. It was the necklace. The chain had been severed, as if cut with a sharp blade – they must have had to slice it from her neck.

Ghilli noticed Avery was awake and leaned forward, reaching to feel her forehead. "Avery, are you okay? You're still a bit clammy. That thing tried to kill you – where on earth did you get it?"

Avery struggled to sit up. Her throat burned. "Cassandra gave it to me," she whispered hoarsely.

"Then you should know that she gave you a gnashing stone, Avery," said Wulver solemnly, taking her hand and feeling for the pulse at her wrist. "A gnashing stone is

160

never a gift. It eats you up from the inside. A witch of her skill would know that."

Avery blinked in bewilderment. "But... Cassandra is trying to help us. She's been sending me things and she knows about Acton and... wait!" Avery looked up suddenly. "Ghilli, it mustn't have been Cassandra. Mab was there when we were leaving and Cassandra was so nervous, she has some sort of hold over her. I think Mab put her up to it, made Cassandra give me the pendant because she knew I would never take anything from her."

"You know Mab and I don't exactly get on, Avery, but giving someone a gnashing stone, that's on a whole other level," said Ghilli. "That's *evil*."

Avery nodded slowly. Having seen what Mab did to the Lammermuirs' castle and the way she had attacked Acton in the tunnel, Avery was convinced that Mab was more than capable of evil. "You suspected her of killing me once, Ghilli. What makes this any different?"

She glanced at Wulver, who was staring hard at her with a strange look on his face. "What? What is it?"

He held up her wrist. "You appear to have a double heartbeat."

Avery started blankly back at him.

"Avery, it seems... Well... it seems that your heart has been bonded with another's."

20

"What do you mean my heart is bonded to someone else's?" Avery looked helplessly between Ghilli and Wulver. "Surely I'd know if something like that had happened to me? Wouldn't I?"

Suddenly the words of the faery with the looped moustache hit her with full force: *In my tale, when Whimbrel heard the prophecy and realised his mistake, they got the young lad's own Cat Fae to share her nine lives with him.*

"So that was how they did it..." said Avery quietly.

"Do you know what happened?" asked Wulver.

She nodded. "I think Acton and I must have bonded hearts so that I could share my nine lives with him, protecting him from Crux Logan's curse."

Ghilli and Wulver glanced at each other in shock.

"The heart is the source of all a person's magic, Avery," said Ghilli, frowning. "Heart bonding isn't done lightly. In the past it was used by those seeking power over another—"

"But where the bonding has been undertaken voluntarily and by equals, one does not control the other,"

Wulver interjected. "They share their magic and whatever powers each may have as individuals."

Avery could see it all clearly now. Whimbrel's plan seemed perfect. Crux's curse might kill Acton once, yet armed with Avery's nine lives he would come back. But somehow this plan hadn't worked. The power of the Beatha Skelpit spell had been too strong, and now Acton was lost somewhere.

Avery felt her shoulders sag under the weight of all this new knowledge.

"I just want to find my wizard," she said sadly. "I just want to find where I belong."

"Then that's what we'll do," said Ghilli, grasping her hand.

"You mean you'll help?" Avery asked.

Ghilli smiled. "Ghilli Dhu and Wulver at your service."

Wulver bowed.

"And me," chirped a familiar voice from the next hammock. Low peeked through the curtain.

Avery leaned forward, heartened to see her friend's freckly face. "Low! You're alright?"

"Yep, I've been given a clean bill of health," Low said cheerily.

"Come on," said Avery eagerly, flinging back the blanket covering her. "We need to get to Baba's safe place and see what else we can find out about Acton."

Ghilli grinned, helping her out of the hammock. "Then there's no time to lose."

Avery pushed Sparrow along Inchmahome's jetty, trying not to bash her shins on the pedals. She found herself scanning the clear night sky above for the distinctive shape of the dragon against the stars. It was a relief that Ghilli and Wulver were coming with them, just in case the creature showed up again.

With his bow and a quiver of arrows slung across his back, Ghilli took the bicycle from Avery as she arrived at the end of the dock, where Wulver, Low, Kest and another faery stallion called Farl waited for her. Ghilli bent down and began tinkering with the bicycle, singing a strange little tune under his breath. Small trails of white sparks fizzed and whizzed around the chain and pedals.

At last he stood up and dusted off his hands. "Okay, Sparrow has agreed to let me and Wulver come along, but won't go against Baba's instructions to keep the destination top secret, so we'll have to follow behind. I've put a little charm on the pedals, all with the bicycle's consent of course, so no one needs to ride it. We can tag along behind on Kest and Farl." He patted Sparrow's saddle. "No offence, but I find a faery horse a more comfortable ride."

Avery pulled her thick travelling cloak around her and leapt lightly behind Wulver onto Farl's back.

Sparrow rose upwards first, pedals spinning. The lamp hanging from the crook of the handlebars flickered on, providing a comforting glow for the group to follow. The horses' hooves kicked up white spray on the loch's surface as they galloped up into the inky sky behind it.

Avery rubbed her throat. It was sore where the gnashing stone had tightened around her neck. What kind of hold must Mab have over Cassandra to make her give Avery such a thing? Avery recalled the pained expression on Cassandra's face when Mab had swept down towards them as they were leaving the library. Poor Cassandra. To do such a thing, even though she had no choice, must have torn her apart inside.

The night air was icy, and Avery sheltered behind Wulver's warm furry back. They were travelling north again. Avery wondered where they were going and what sort of safe place Baba had in mind for them. In spite of the light from the moon she couldn't make anything out on the ground except the odd silver ribbon of a river or the shimmer of a loch. It was only when Wulver pointed them out that she realised the looming shadows ahead were mountains.

"Do they have a name, Wulver?" asked Avery.

"Those are the Cairngorm Mountains. That's where I was born."

"Are your family still there?"

"No," Wulver replied after a pause. "The magic has thinned too much here for werewolves to survive. There are rumours of an isolated pack who hide themselves away in the Cape Wrath area, but most emigrated to eastern Europe in the 1800s. As far as I know, I'm the last werewolf in Scotland."

"Will you leave too?"

"I have cousins in Romania, but no, I don't think so. I love Inchmahome. It's my home."

"For as long as I can remember I've wanted somewhere to really belong," confided Avery. "Bob and Cindy, my guardians, tried their best, but I've always felt… incomplete somehow. It's lonely being the last of your kind, isn't it?"

"It must be worse for you though," Wulver said. "You really are the last of your kind… anywhere."

"I'm starting to wonder if that's true," she replied thoughtfully. "Since this all started, I've met all sorts of people who feel the same way I do about the world. People like you, Ghilli and Cassandra. People who are kind and believe in truth and standing up for a better world. Maybe I am the last of the Cat Fae, but I'm not the last of other kinds of people. Maybe there are lots of ways of belonging."

Wulver reached forward and patted Farl's neck. "That's a comforting idea, Avery."

They continued the rest of the journey in silence, each deep in their own thoughts.

21

It was only by the salty tang on the air and the sound of crashing waves that Avery realised they had reached the coast. The wide expanse of the North Sea appeared, glittering beneath them with the reflected light of the moon. It wasn't long until she could make out the dark shapes of a group of islands that grew bigger with each hoofbeat.

"The Orkneys," said Wulver, peering down. "We're off the north coast of Scotland."

"Orkney is where the Stones live," called Ghilli. "They're giants. I bet that's where Baba was sending you for safety."

Low shot Avery a panicked look. Avery had to admit that giants didn't sound very safe to her either.

Slowing to a canter, the horses followed the glow of Sparrow's lamp and descended onto an exposed piece of grassy headland, halting just short of an enormous standing stone. Avery and Low dismounted, looking at Ghilli uneasily.

"Where are they?" she whispered.

Ghilli nodded at the stone. "Right there. You'll have to speak to Watch before you can speak to the others. And whatever you do, call him 'Mr Stone' until he says otherwise."

"What? Stone is his surname?" asked Low.

"Yes, they're all Stones. Brothers I think, but no one knows for sure. They're so old I don't think they even know."

Ghilli was interrupted by a loud grating sound and a deep rumble of the earth under their feet that nearly knocked them all to the ground. The stone was moving, turning towards them. Before she knew it, Avery was looking at several haphazardly sewn knee patches on two enormous denim-clad legs. Her eyes travelled upwards past a brass belt buckle and a pair of red braces, eventually reaching a giant craggy face with huge shaggy eyebrows and twinkly eyes.

"Who goes there?" he boomed in a deep baritone.

"Hello, Watch!" called Ghilli. "I've brought Avery Buckle, last of the Cat Fae. Baba sent her here for safe-keeping. I guess she'll need to see Odin."

"Alright, Ghilli. No need to shout." The giant shook his head. "I know I'm a long way up for you littlies but there's nothing wrong with my hearing. Pitch perfect I am!"

He peered down at Avery with interest and scratched his head. "Last of the Cat Fae, eh? Well, well."

"Hello, Mr Stone." Avery tried to resist the impulse to shout. His head really did seem such a long way up.

"Pleased to make your acquaintance," the giant said with a smile. "Call me Watch." Then he folded his arms, all friendliness gone. "But I'm not letting you through to Odin without the password."

"Oh come on, Watch," protested Ghilli. "Baba sent Avery here. You must be expecting her, and besides, it's me, Ghilli. You know me!"

The giant frowned. "There's danger everywhere these days, Ghilli Dhu. The faeries know that more than most." He looked suspiciously over his shoulder and out into the dark night before leaning forward. "Can't trust anyone."

Ghilli gave the giant a withering look, but Watch just folded his arms tighter and raised his massive shaggy eyebrows. "No password, no entry!"

Watch's shirtsleeves were rolled up, revealing two muscly forearms, covered in blue tattoos. Ghilli didn't seem at all nervous of the giant but Avery's knees were knocking.

Ghilli shook his head. "Oh, alright then. Let me think..." He looked up at the stars for a moment in concentration.

"Ha! Got it!" he said, clicking his fingers. "Scotch snap."

Watch looked crestfallen. "How on earth did you get that?"

"Because, as if it isn't plain enough to see, I am actually the same Ghilli Dhu you've known for years," retorted the faery with a roll of his eyes.

The giant rubbed his stubbled chin then seemed to make up his mind. "Alright, you'd better follow me."

He turned and stomped off, scratching his head in a bemused sort of way. Ghilli, Wulver, Low and Avery jogged to keep up.

"Is Scotch snap a special sort of game they play up here?" panted Low.

"No, it's a musical term," replied Ghilli with a laugh. "You get it in Scottish fiddle playing. Watch invented it. The Stones love their music."

They followed Watch into the centre of a ring, made up of five huge standing stones. His giant legs had brought him there faster than they could run, so they only caught the end of his introduction.

"… therefore, I present to you the last of the Cat Fae, Avery Buckle," he said, sweeping a huge arm in Avery's direction.

With a now familiar rumbling sound, the five stones turned towards Avery. They were a motley lot, mostly bearded, and adorned with an array of earrings and tattoos. If it hadn't been that their weight would have sunk any ship in seconds, they would easily have passed for a band of scallywag pirates.

The largest spoke first. "And who have you brought with you, Avery Buckle, last of the Cat Fae?"

"This is Ghilli Dhu, Mr Stone. I think you might know him already," she began nervously. "This is Wulver, and this is Low."

"Indeed." The craggy giant stroked his long grey beard thoughtfully. "Well, I am Odin Stone – you can call me Odin. I received Baba's message, but we expected you yesterday. From the look on your face I don't think you went off for a jig and a caper, so where have you been?"

Avery sighed. "It's a bit of a long story."

Odin slapped his thigh and threw back his head with a roar of laughter. "Hear that, boys? A long story!"

The other giants fell about laughing, clutching their sides. Avery looked at Low in astonishment. This wasn't what she had been expecting from a group of giants. What was so funny? Low shrugged back at her.

"Giant humour!" Ghilli explained, rolling his eyes.

After a few awkward minutes the giants regained their composure. Wiping away tears from his eyes with a bedsheet-sized handkerchief he pulled from his shirt pocket, Odin said, "Right then. You'd better fill us in."

Odin listened patiently as Avery told them of their journey so far, and about needing to find Acton. He stroked his wiry beard and occasionally fiddled with the gold hoop in his left ear. When she'd finished he put his hands on his hips. "Well, we know Acton, don't we, lads?" he exclaimed.

His brothers all nodded in agreement. "Oh, aye!"

"You do?" asked Avery incredulously. She could hardly believe her ears. They knew Acton!

"Oh yes!" replied Odin proudly. "Us giants don't forget. Acton's been up here plenty of times."

"This is brilliant!" said Ghilli, leaping forward. "He hasn't been wiped out completely then. Do you know how we can find him?"

"Oh aye, lad," said Odin, beaming confidently. "Now let me see. Well, he's... now hang on. It'll come to me... Yes, he left something here for us to keep safe. Wait a minute. Tiny, fiddly thing it was. We were to pass it on at the right time, but dear me..." The giant scratched his head. "I can't seem to remember!"

22

Odin blinked, a mystified look on his face. "While I'm thinking on it, I can't be at all certain that Acton *was* here. Lads?" Odin turned to his brothers for help, but they looked at each other in confusion.

"No, can't be sure," they chorused.

"You see! This is exactly what's happening everywhere," said Avery, disappointed. "Nobody can remember. She's wiping out all traces of him."

"Mr Odin Stone, sir," interjected Low, hopping anxiously from foot to foot. He pointed up at Odin's shirt pocket. "Up there. Is that it? The thing you were meant to pass on? It's got Avery's name on it."

Everyone stopped and followed Low's finger up to Odin's shirt pocket, into which he had hastily re-stuffed his handkerchief.

"This tiddly thing?" asked Odin, squinting at an envelope tucked in behind. "I've had that for some time now, but blow me if I can remember how I came by it. And now you mention it, I think it *was* the thing I was supposed to keep safe until I could pass it on."

The envelope was about the size of a pillowcase but looked tiny between the giant's massive thumb and finger as he passed it down to Avery. She took hold of it with both hands, a familiar warm feeling flooding her heart. Trying to steady her breathing, she focused on the swirling handwriting on the envelope. It was exactly the same as the writing on the other packages she had been sent. The name along the top of the envelope read: *Avery*.

"So that's you then," said Odin peering through a pair of wonky reading glasses at the envelope and then staring down at her.

Low came and stood by Avery's side. "Are you going to open it?"

Avery nodded, and with trembling hands she peeled back the flap. At first there didn't seem to be anything inside. She felt right to the bottom. It was definitely empty. But when she pulled out her hand it was covered in what looked to be black coal dust. It briefly sparked with a crackle, like burning embers on an open fire.

As Avery looked up in confusion at Low, the world around her turned into a blur of moonlight and shadows. To Low, she appeared to freeze on the spot, just as she had during the other visions, but for Avery, she felt as though she were being flung far up into the star-studded sky. Her brain desperately tried to locate which way was up and which was down as she tumbled, but it was no good. Then the atmosphere seemed to change and, with confusion, she saw that the sun was rising above golden hills. She definitely wasn't in the Orkneys any more. And she was approaching the ground – fast!

All of her cat reflexes kicked in, and she deftly landed in a tuft of thick moorland grass just a few metres away from a small stone building. Nearby, there stood a castle complete with turrets and towers, the stone walls the colour of honey in the early morning light. Even through her dizziness, Avery could see that the landscape and the castle looked oddly familiar. The smaller building too. It was the Lammermuirs' gatehouse, just the way Knuckle had described it before Mab destroyed it. Smoke rose lazily from the chimney.

Someone was home.

Avery walked uncertainly towards the weather-beaten wooden door, and with a deep breath gave it a brisk rap.

"Door's open!" came a hearty call. "Come in!"

Inside the gatehouse, flagstones covered the floor and a fire blazed in the hearth. A glass skylight took up most of the roof, filling the room with the glow of the rising sun. A sweet scent filled the air, wafting from a peach tree growing in a large terracotta pot in the corner. Its branches embraced the roof space, ripe fruit dripping from the boughs.

A young man with broad shoulders, sun-kissed skin and caramel-coloured hair sat in an armchair by the fire.

Avery took in his navy waistcoat covered in geometric patterns, and his red scarf dotted with white mice. She recognised him straight away from her vision in the tunnel.

"Acton!"

He jumped to his feet when he saw her, his face creasing into the most wonderful smile.

Avery ran to him, burying herself in his welcoming hug. Everything about him was comfortingly familiar, from the smell of his clothes to the sound of his voice. It was like suddenly remembering some long-forgotten dream. Right there in that moment, she knew she'd come home. She knew she belonged – with Acton.

"You've come a long way. Would you like a drink?" he asked.

He pulled up a second chair by the fire and she sat down gladly, her tail curling over the edge of the chair.

Acton reached for a chipped jug and poured out a mugful of creamy milk for Avery before settling himself back in his chair. "Odin gave you the envelope, then? Has he played the fiddle for you yet? There's not a better bunch of musicians the world over. I've had many a good night with them."

Avery shook her head. "No, not yet. We've just arrived." She peered into her mug. "Am I having another vision? I've never been able to talk to anyone in visions before, or… drink things." She sipped the milk hesitantly. It tasted real.

Acton chuckled. "Your ability to have visions comes from me. I shared it with you when we bonded hearts, but it's weak at the moment because my magic is weak. This vision is different to any others you might have experienced. I set this one up before, when my powers were strong."

Avery gazed at him. She could hardly believe he was actually here, in front of her.

"I put a spell on the coal dust from Knuckle's hearth here," he continued. "That's what was in the envelope. When you touched it, it brought you back here, to me. That's why you're able to talk to me." He gave a smile. "And taste the milk."

He leaned back, regarding her. "You looked older the last time I saw you. I think you must have passed through one or two lives since then."

"Am... Am I very different?" she asked, suddenly uneasy. She had never really thought about whether she might have been different in her other lives.

He smiled again. "I would know you anywhere, Avery. And the fact that you're here means you must have received my other packages: the guidebook, the sea glass and the peach stone?"

Avery nodded. So it was Acton, not Cassandra, who had sent them!

"Excellent." Acton's brow furrowed. "However, that also means that she has started on her final plans to wake the Crannog. I arranged for the parcels to be released to you once she made her move. Magic must have thinned enough for her to push forward, then. She has discovered how to wake the beast?"

"Yes, I think so." Avery could almost smell the smoke-filled library as she remembered. "She smashed your father's memory casket and murdered the book inside to get it."

"All those precious memories, gone." Acton sighed sadly. "But more importantly, this means there's no time to lose – the Crannog will destroy everything in its path, Avery. And everyone." He looked at her grimly. "It's up to us to make sure that beast is never woken."

23

"But I don't understand how she thinks she can control the Crannog once she's woken it." Avery gripped the armrests of her chair at the thought of waking the monstrous creature currently slumbering under Edinburgh.

Acton threw a log onto the fire. "Heart-bond magic, the same as the kind we use to share your nine lives. Though not quite. She has misused the magic to bond with other creatures before in order to take control of them, and believes she can do the same with the Crannog."

Avery's eyes widened as she remembered Ghilli's words on Inchmahome about the dark side of heart bonding. "What other creatures?"

"The ollipheist is one," said Acton. "It's a dragon, really. A serpent that can fly. The bond means she can appear as dragon or human."

"One attacked me and my friend Low!"

"Indeed?" Acton paused. "You know, once I believed she might be different. I truly loved her for a time. But in the end she was a Logan through and through." He shook his head bitterly. "The point is, Avery, the heart bond between you and I is equal and in balance, but the Logans have always sought greater power. Crux Logan believed he was strong enough to control the Crannog, and his daughter has fallen into the same trap. No heart is strong enough to control it. But we must hurry, Avery. You won't have long here. You have to go back."

Avery blanched. "Aren't you coming? You're the one who knows how to stop her! Now I've found you, you're going to come with me, right?"

Acton shook his head. "I'm already there, Avery."

"I don't understand!" replied Avery, panic filling her.

He gave her a sad smile. "You're talking to an old version of me, Avery. I suspected I would be in danger if I refused to help her. I knew she would kill me. So I used my magic to prepare this vision and the parcels for you. As clues. I also knew my heart bond with you was strong. It stopped the spell from destroying me completely. Though it took time for my magic to gather itself, and you lived another life in the meantime, our bond brought me back to a place where I was once very happy. I won't look quite the same, but I'm there. You saved me, Avery. I'm alive in your time. I've come back, just like you did."

Avery leaned forward. "This doesn't make sense. I don't understand what you mean. Where are you?"

Acton didn't answer. Instead he looked up at the skylight and around the cottage. "You and I used to come here every summer with my friend Kentigern Lammermuir. His family built it. We had such wonderful times here; I only wish you could remember them." He looked down at his hands, speaking softly to himself. "I wonder what has become of our memory casket."

Avery stared at him. She couldn't make sense of what he was saying.

Looking up again, he smiled thoughtfully. "We will have happy times again, Avery. I've seen it. But I've also seen that you're going to need to fight for them. To fight for the future."

Avery's heart was at war with her head. She wanted to stay here, with him. She didn't want to let go of this vision and fight for anything. But she knew she had to.

"Okay," she said solemnly. "But I don't understand how we stop her."

"You know the whole story, Avery: you need to tell everyone who has forgotten."

"But I've tried that!" Avery protested. "No one remembers, they don't understand!"

The distant sound of a merry jig being played on a fiddle began to float through the open window.

"No one understands?" Acton asked, reaching for a peach from a branch above his head. He tossed it in the air and caught it easily. "Are you sure about that?"

Avery thought. Acton was right. Low understood, and Ghilli, and Wulver.

Avery looked at him. The way he threw the peach up and caught it sparked something in her mind.

The fiddle playing was getting louder. Avery put her hands over her ears, trying to think. She had seen someone toss a peach stone like that...

She turned to Acton quickly. "You said you're already there?"

He nodded encouragingly.

"You've been reborn, just like I have each time Mab killed me?" If only she could stop that fiddle music and think.

Acton frowned. "Mab?" he repeated, but his voice was fading. The music became deafening and the gatehouse began to disappear, Acton with it.

"No, Avery, it's not—" Acton cried out, but she couldn't hear him any more. She was tumbling once again into moonlight and shadows.

"I know where you are, Acton!" she shouted into the darkness. "I'm going to go and get you, and together we're going to stop Mab!"

24

Avery opened her eyes to find herself back in the centre of the giant stone circle. Here the music that had interrupted her vision of the Lammermuirs' gatehouse was in full flow. Odin, eyes closed, tapped his foot as he fiddled, while his brothers accompanied him on guitars, a double bass and a hand drum. A bonfire crackled, its flames licking the base of a huge pot of steaming stew.

"Avery!" Low ran towards her. "She's back!" he shouted to the others.

The giants put down their instruments and everyone gathered round her.

"What happened?" asked Low eagerly. "You froze again."

"I saw Acton!" Avery said, shaking her head at Watch, who was trying to hand her a bowl of broth. "No thank you, Watch. I can't eat, I've got so much to tell you."

"Go on then," said Odin.

"I know where my wizard is!" she said excitedly. "As soon as the old Acton threw that peach, I knew.

Acton is Tab! He was reborn at the Lammermuirs' –
somewhere he thought was safe – except it's now the most
dangerous place he could be!" Avery relayed everything
Acton had told her as the others listened, open-mouthed.
She paused for breath, eyes alight. "We need to go and
get him, now! Before Mab discovers who he really is. And
then we need to stop her waking the Crannog!"

"You could be right, Avery," said Ghilli. "But I don't
think we should go anywhere tonight."

"What are you talking about? We have to! What if
Mab goes to the castle and finds Tab?" demanded Avery.

"I agree with Ghilli," said Wulver. "And now we know
the dragon was probably Mab coming for you, it wouldn't
be wise to travel at night."

"Are you serious?" Avery couldn't believe how cautious
everyone was being. "We're talking about the end of
the world as we know it. One night might make all the
difference!"

"It isn't safe." Ghilli folded his arms across his chest.
"If you're right, at the moment we're the only ones who
know where Acton is. If we set off tonight it's the perfect
opportunity for Mab to pick us off, and then who's going
to save the world?"

"Listen to them, Avery," added Odin. "You can head
off at first light."

Avery sighed moodily.

Watch offered her the bowl of stew again. "Cullen skink. It's my own recipe. Best fish stew for miles."

"It is very good," nodded Low, patting his tummy.

She glared at him but took it, grumpily gulping down big mouthfuls until the warmth of the food in her stomach began to melt her irritation.

Watch banked up the fire and brought out piles of enormous tartan blankets while the other giants began packing away their instruments. As Avery and Low made themselves beds on the ground, Odin lifted his head to the sky. One hand on his chest, his eyes closed, he started to sing. His voice was rich and powerful.

He sang of a Cat Fae searching for her lost wizard, and of a terrible witch who wanted to wake an ancient evil beast and rule the world. Avery and Low listened to him, mesmerised, tingles running up and down their spines. When he finished there was deep silence. Odin nodded and looked down at Avery.

"There, Avery Buckle. I have sung your story into legend. That should jolt a few memories up and down Scotland."

Avery snuggled down, exhausted. Tucked up in a blanket beside her, Low wriggled his toes, and then glanced over at her anxiously.

"What is it?" she asked. "Go on, you can tell me."

"Well…" He hesitated. "It's really great that you're going to find Acton and that you have this special bond, but…"

Avery rolled onto her side and looked at him. "Low, you're my best friend in all the world. Nothing, not even a heart bond, is going to change that."

"Well then," Low smiled and awkwardly smoothed down his blanket before quickly changing the subject, "I really hope giants don't snore."

It was lucky they had bedded down close to the fire because an icy frost covered the landscape the next morning. Avery peeked over the edge of her blanket. Wulver and Ghilli were already awake, carrying bundles of wood they had collected to build up the fire again.

Avery sat up, the memories of her vision the night before rushing back to her. "What time is it? We need to go!"

"Don't panic," Ghilli replied. "It's early yet. Breakfast is almost ready."

The morning was bright and crisp, the sky a pretty pale blue as the sea lapped at the shore. Avery stood up, jumping up and down to warm herself. It was only then that she realised the giants had gone. Instead, a circle of enormous standing stones towered over the spot where they had slept.

"Dey wurn ack oo own," spat Low, landing beside her before quickly turning back into a boy.

"You what?" she asked.

"Sorry," replied Low, removing a stick from his mouth that he'd been carrying between his teeth. "I've been flying about collecting firewood."

"You've got hands, y'know," said Avery.

"I know." Low grinned. "It just feels nice carrying sticks in my mouth. A bit owly. I wonder if there are any nest-building books in the library…"

Avery gave him an exasperated look. "What were you trying to say?"

"Oh yes. The giants. Apparently they turned back to stone." He leaned forward and whispered, "Although Ghilli said to watch what we say because they can still hear."

Avery looked at the massive grey stones. How long had they been here, these strange creatures living this extraordinary half-life?

"Don't you think it's funny, Low?" asked Avery.

"What's that?" he replied.

"This magical world we're experiencing, and the ordinary world. It's all interwoven, but nobody in the ordinary world knows a thing."

Low stopped. "I think people do know, in their own way," he said. "When I think of all the times I've felt a shiver down my spine, or thought I've seen something out of the corner of my eye. I wonder now, what might it have been? Maybe a faery or witch passing by.

It's quite comforting really, knowing that there's more to the real world than meets the eye."

He turned away, their conversation interrupted by Ghilli's call: "Come on you two, breakfast's ready!"

They stood beside the fire holding steaming mugs of hot tea in their hands. Ghilli buttered thick slices of spiced bread and handed them out.

"So where are we heading?" he asked.

"The Lammermuirs' castle first," said Avery, taking a sip of her tea. "We need to find Tab and then head back to the library to stop Mab."

"Have you any idea where exactly this castle is, Avery?" asked Ghilli. "Or how to get there?"

She looked at him. How could she have been so stupid? In her haste to get back to Knuckle's gatehouse, she hadn't thought of that. She had no idea where it was!

"Maybe the sea glass might show us again," Low suggested hopefully.

Avery pulled it from her pocket but the glass remained frosted and dull.

"I believe you require a cloudy day, or to be travelling at night for a sun stone to work," said Wulver, looking up at the clear, bright skies. There wasn't a cloud to be seen.

There was a sudden clattering sound and they all

turned to see Baba's bicycle spinning its wheels and flashing its lamp. Kest whinnied.

"Of course!" cried Ghilli. "Sparrow knows the way!"

They quickly finished their breakfast, stamped out the fire and piled up the tartan blankets beside one of the stones. Within minutes the blankets had turned into a bundle of hay, picked up and scattered by a sudden breeze.

The four of them climbed onto the horses' backs and took off into the sky, following Sparrow's spinning pedals. Avery looked down on the standing stones. "Goodbye!" she called out. "And thank you!"

As they slowly gained height, she thought she caught the faintest hint of fiddle music on the wind.

25

This time their journey to the castle was in daylight so Avery had a clear view of the landscape as they travelled. Mountains, forests, rivers and lochs sped past in a patchwork of purples and greens and blues. Faery horse was surely the best way to travel. But with the rise and fall of Farl's gallop, Avery's emotions seesawed. One minute she couldn't stop herself from smiling; everything was going to be okay now she had finally found her wizard. Then in the next she couldn't help but question herself: how much did Tab know about his past? What if he didn't believe her and wanted nothing to do with her?

At last the horses descended, following the glow of Sparrow's lamp through a thick mist and landing in front of the tall gates. The swirling ironwork dripped with moisture. Everything was silent and still. Ghostly.

"What a peculiar place," said Ghilli, gazing up at the gates and putting his hand out to touch them. "Avery, I thought you said there was a message about betrayal in the archway. It just says 'Lammermuir Castle. True courage lies within'. That must be the family's clan motto."

Avery came to stand beside him. Her heart was thudding in her chest. Suddenly she was reluctant to push the gates open, all her doubts about Tab's reaction to what she would say crowding out her hope.

"Let me try," she said, reaching out a trembling hand. As her fingers connected with the cold metal, the letters in the archway rearranged themselves to show the secret words she and Low had read on their first visit.

"There must be something about you that reveals them," said Wulver thoughtfully. "Perhaps it's because of your connection to Acton through the heart bond."

Avery barely heard him. What if Mab had already been here and discovered who Tab really was? She felt a gentle hand clasp her own. It was Low.

"Come on," he said. "Shall we go through together?"

She nodded numbly and they pushed open the gates.

On the other side, the blackened ruins of the castle loomed out of the mist, strange and desolate. Nearer at hand, a thin ribbon of smoke rose from the chimney of the collapsed gatehouse.

Avery saw him immediately, rounding a pile of rubble, his mop of hair flopping down into his face as he concentrated on carrying a bundle of firewood. Tab looked up in surprise, then they locked eyes, and he smiled.

"Avery! Low! You came back." He dropped the

firewood and ran towards them, calling over his shoulder, "Knuckle, Avery and Low are here. Come and see!"

Knuckle's head popped out of the entrance to the collapsed gatehouse. "Still no adequate parental supervision I can see!" he growled, but Avery thought she detected a pleased note in his voice.

"It's so good to see you again." Tab pulled Avery and Low in for an excited hug. "And who's this?"

"This is Ghilli," explained Low. "He's a faery."

"'Wow, I've never met a faery. Pleased to meet you, Ghilli." Tab pumped Ghilli's hand.

"The pleasure's all mine," replied Ghilli, grinning.

"And you're a werewolf, that I can see." Tab turned to Wulver. "I've always wondered, is it very hot in summer having that much fur?"

"Fortunately, that's not something I have to worry about too much in Scottish summers. I'm Wulver," he replied, shaking Tab's small hand in his large furry one. "We've had quite a journey to find you."

"Find me?"

Wulver turned to Avery. "Perhaps it's best if you take it from here…"

Avery took a deep breath, nerves fizzing in her stomach. She was about to launch into the explanation she'd tried to put together in her head on the journey there, but Knuckle interrupted.

"You should come inside," he called from the gatehouse, his gaze fixed on the mist-filled sky. "It's not safe to be out in the open."

"He's right," said Tab, bending down and picking up a stray peach stone, one of the many that littered the ground. He tossed it up in the air and caught it again easily. His gesture took Avery back to the old gatehouse, and the old Acton, in her vision, watching a thrown peach rise and fall in the air.

"Please, don't go inside just yet," she blurted. "If I don't say what I've got to say now, I don't think I ever will." Avery looked at Tab. "This is going to sound ridiculous, but… your name isn't Tab, it's Acton Baxter, and you're a wizard – in fact, you're *my* wizard!" The words had come tumbling out, and they hung suspended in the air for a moment before Knuckle's voice broke the silence.

"Well of course he's Acton Baxter. And of course he's a wizard. We knew that."

"I don't understand. You called him Tab," said Avery, looking from Knuckle to Acton in bewilderment.

"Yes," said Knuckle, speaking slowly, as if she were very stupid. "But I don't believe we ever said that was his *name*. Tab's just what I called him because that witch from Cunningfoot – can't remember her name, haven't seen her in a long time – she came to me when I found the lad as a baby and said I had to keep him hidden, that he was

193

important to the survival of the magical world, no less! I tried out a few different names, but after the vomiting incident with the tablet I thought Tab was quite apt." He gave Acton a wry grin.

"Wait, a witch? What witch?" Avery felt like she might burst into tears. She couldn't process any more. One of the witches had known all along that Acton was here? It certainly couldn't have been Mab…

"Don't you see, Avery?" asked Ghilli, putting a kind hand on her shoulder. "It doesn't matter who it was. They will have forgotten all about it because of the Beatha Skelpit spell."

"Beatha Skelpit spell?" Knuckle's forehead scrunched in confusion. "What's that got to do with the lad?"

Avery shook her head in frustration. "There's no time to explain!"

Acton moved closer to Avery and took both of her hands in his, calming her thoughts. "I don't know anything about any spell. All I know is that I'm a wizard. And I'm not even sure of that part really. I mean, I can't even do magic. But Avery, I *do* know that everything you've said is true. I can feel it here." He tapped his chest. "I think I felt it the moment I saw you. Saying goodbye to you was the hardest thing I've ever had to do."

Tears rolled down Avery's cheeks but she was smiling. She felt it too. Deep in her heart, she knew it.

At last, she was home.

Acton squeezed her hand. "Perhaps now that everything is out in the open, I can go back to my real name. Maybe everyone could call me Acton from now on?"

Avery nodded. "Okay, Tab. I mean Acton!"

Low sniffed loudly, his glasses steamed up with tears. Wulver put an arm around him. Ghilli pretended he was too cool for crying, but his bottom lip trembled. Behind Acton, a puff of glittering embers shot up in the sky as Knuckle blew his nose noisily in his handkerchief. "Well now, I think a cup of tea is in order. I'll go and put the kettle on—"

"No, we have to go!" cried Avery, wiping her eyes. "We have to get back to Edinburgh." She looked to Acton. "I can explain on the way, but we've got to stop Mab, we've got to make people remember you, before it's too late. Will you help me?"

Acton simply grinned. "Do I get to ride Sparrow?"

26

Farl and Kest's hooves clattered down on the pavement outside the library. As usual, passersby didn't seem to notice the odd assortment of characters who had just landed in Edinburgh city centre with flying horses and a magical bicycle in tow.

Letting Sparrow lead the way, Avery and Acton had ridden back to Edinburgh behind Ghilli and Wulver, with Low soaring beside them. He was growing more confident in his flying skills. Avery had explained to Acton as best she could about Mab, the Beatha Skelpit spell and the Crannog, although she wasn't sure how much of it he had actually taken in. Never having been beyond the castle gates before, he'd spent most of their journey staring wide-eyed as the rolling hills gave way to the tumbling rooftops of Edinburgh. Now he and the others all pounded on the great library door.

"Edgar, open up!" shouted Ghilli.

The shutter opened with a brisk motion and Edgar's many eyes peered out anxiously. Acton audibly gulped.

"It's okay," Avery reassured him. "Edgar's our friend."

"Edgar, we really need to speak to the witches," she pleaded. "It's about Mab."

Edgar unbolted the door and stood back to let them in. "But only Miss Mab is here, gathering potions to take down to Canonmills. That's where the other witches are – there are legions of Badoch gathering!"

"What?" exclaimed Avery.

"They started appearing last night and by this morning there were thousands of them," explained Edgar fretfully, taking Sparrow from Avery and leaning the bicycle up against the lobby wall. "Glaurt and the other witches have gone down to send them back to the mountains once and for all."

"And Mab is here on her own?" asked Avery hurriedly.

"Yes, but she's going to join them as soon as she's got what she needs," said Edgar, suddenly peevish. "Miss Mab's no coward, if that's what you're thinking."

Avery turned to the others, her face full of urgency. "We've got to stop her from leaving the library."

"Let's not hang about then," cried Ghilli. "Come on!"

"Stop her? I don't understand!" wailed Edgar, wringing his hands as they ran past him and up the corridor.

There wasn't a soul in the library. They hurtled up the grand staircase, running past empty rooms and rows of still bookshelves. It was almost eerie. There was no sign of Mab anywhere. The place was silent, like the library itself was holding its breath. The only sound was the fall of their hurried footsteps as they made their way to the stationery cupboard. One of the strip lights overhead flickered like a warning signal as they slowed and cautiously approached. The cupboard doors were open.

The group gathered outside, peering into the dim interior.

"She's in there," whispered Ghilli. "I can hear someone moving about."

He was right. There was the distinct sound of swishing robes, the jangle of keys and the clink of glass bottles coming from inside the cupboard. It sounded as though Mab was the other side of Cunningfoot's front door, preparing to leave.

"Let's just shut her in," hissed Low, obviously eager to avoid coming to blows with the witch if at all possible.

Ghilli nodded, carefully shoving away the piles of books that were precariously keeping the stationery cupboard doors open with his foot. Wulver edged the doors closed, gesturing for them all to gather bits of furniture to barricade Mab inside.

Acton was passing Ghilli another chair to add to the pile when the cupboard door handle suddenly started to jiggle, and then to shake. There was the sound of muffled cursing and a thud, as if someone had kicked the door from inside. Then the thudding got louder and a dent appeared.

"I don't like this," whispered Low, stepping slowly backwards, his eyes glued to the door.

"I don't think it's going to hold her," said Ghilli, wincing.

There was another thud, and the doorframe began to splinter.

Avery shook her head. "If only the other witches were here, we could tell them what Mab has done. They would stop her!"

At that moment there was a flurry of sparks and a loud **BANG!** as the door of the stationery cupboard blew off and a furious Mab exploded out into the library.

"What is the meaning of this?" she bellowed. Then her eyes alighted on Avery. "You?!"

Mab's eyes blazed, and in her anger her red hair seemed to take on a life of its own, twisting in the air like tentacles. It reminded Avery of the tendrils around the dragon's snout as it had chased them in the skies above Inchmahome.

Avery gulped, her courage deserting her under Mab's fearsome gaze. Then she sensed someone at her shoulder. Acton was there, his gaze fixed resolutely on Mab. Avery felt someone brush against her other shoulder, and saw that Low had moved to be by her side.

Ghilli and Wulver shifted to stand close behind her too. Surrounded by friends, Avery found her courage returning, and with it her voice.

"We won't let you leave this library, Mab!"

The witch's eyes narrowed and she pursed her thin lips. Avery could almost feel the effort it took for Mab to contain her rage. She spoke calmly, but there was an icy edge to her voice.

"Avery, move aside. You have no idea what you are meddling in!"

"That's exactly it, Mab. We do know. We know all about it!" Avery clenched her fists. "We know how you tried to destroy Acton Baxter and how you used the Beatha Skelpit spell. That's why you've been killing books: so everyone would forget him." Avery gestured to Acton. "Except you've failed. We found him, and we're going to make sure everyone knows it."

"Ridiculous!" spat Mab. "I have no idea who this boy is, and I would never use such magic. I—"

"You're going to try and deny it when we've got evidence?" Avery's blood was up now. She wasn't going to let Mab lie her way out of it. "My heart bond with Acton meant that you had to kill me so that you could finally finish him off. You've been hunting me through my lives while pretending to take care of me. You even tried again when we were on the way to Inchmahome, coming after us in your dragon form."

"Out of my way—"

"I knew you didn't take the faery attacks seriously," Ghilli butted in. "I should have known that you couldn't be trusted."

"Insolent young faery!" growled Mab.

Avery blinked. Something strange was happening. Mab seemed to be getting taller. But Avery ignored the alarm bells ringing inside her head, telling her to be careful. She was determined to stop Mab, once and for all.

"We know you're planning to wake the Crannog under Edinburgh," Avery pushed on. "That's why the Badoch are down at Canonmills. So you can complete what your father started. You're a Logan through and through!"

Avery delivered her parting shot, arms folded across her chest. But she hadn't been imagining it, Mab *was* growing taller. The witch's robes billowed out around her, her fiery hair coiling and twisting like a nest of snakes. Avery could feel the powerful thrum of magic in the air as the library became dark and cold around them. Mab's fingertips glowed red with spells and she glared thunderously down at Avery.

"I am running out of time. Move. Aside!" Her voice was thick with threat.

Avery quailed. What else could they do to stop her? There had to be something!

Suddenly a bright spark shot out over Avery's head and hit Mab with full force. The witch froze instantly, like a statue, her writhing hair suspended mid-air. Misfiring spells shot from her fingers, but fizzled away into nothing.

Avery blinked. What had just happened? Something had stopped Mab in her tracks.

"Um…"

Everyone turned to look at Acton, who was staring down at his fingers in shock. His voice trembled. "Um… so that's never happened before."

"You cast a spell, Acton, and just in the nick of time!" Ghilli's voice was full of relief, but it shook slightly too. It had been a close call.

"Of course! You're a wizard, that's what you do!" cried Avery, beaming at him.

"How long does it last?" Low asked, cautiously waving his arms in front of Mab to check she really couldn't move.

"She wasn't going to listen, and when Avery was saying all the terrible things she had done, I could feel this strange bubbling inside me." Acton was laughing now. "I think it's you, Avery. Now we're together again, I can do magic."

"Well, it was the perfect moment to discover your magical abilities," said Wulver.

Avery grinned. "And now we've stopped Mab raising the Crannog, all we need to do is go down to Canonmills and help the witches defeat the Badoch. We've won! We've really won!"

Everyone started laughing then and grinning big broad smiles. Low jumped to give Ghilli a high-five.

"Someone will need to stay and stand guard over Mab," interjected Wulver, thinking of practicalities.

"It had better be you, Acton," said Ghilli. "You might only be able to do one spell at the moment, but that one spell is more powerful than anything any of us can do."

"Oh," said Avery, reluctant to leave Acton behind. She'd only just found him; she didn't want to risk losing him again.

"Sorry, Avery." Ghilli gave an apologetic smile and turned to Acton. "Your magic is new, so that spell will likely wear off after a bit and you'll need to re-cast it again quickly."

Acton nodded. "It's okay. This is the most useful place I can be." He bumped his shoulder against Avery's. "Once this is all over we'll have loads of time together. Now go!"

Avery, Low, Ghilli and Wulver ran back through the library to the entrance, where Edgar was still wringing his hands, his face full of concern.

"Don't worry, Edgar," said Ghilli, slapping him on the back. "You're safe now. Mab's frozen solid upstairs and Acton has enough power to keep her that way."

"But-but-but…" stuttered Edgar.

"We can't stop," interrupted Avery. "We've got to go and help the others get rid of the Badoch!"

"But-but…" Edgar glanced anxiously between them and the staircase up into the library. "Oh dear, oh dear!"

"It's all going to be okay, Edgar," cried Avery as they hurried out onto the pavement. "You'll see!"

They saw the columns of black smoke rising up from Canonmills as soon as they flew over the Royal Mile. Ghilli and Wulver urged Kest and Farl on, but both horses reared onto their hind legs in dread as they reached the top of the ridge that led down to the park.

Everywhere the writhing black forms of the Badoch lurked. Not only in the park, but on the surrounding rooftops too, creeping around chimneystacks and feeling the cracks of doors and windows with their claws. They licked the air with their long black tongues as if tasting the threat of violence that hung heavily over the park. The sound of their terrible snarls filled the air and thrummed in Avery's eardrums.

In the middle of the park, the Badoch massed the tightest, writhing around the figures of the witches. They had arranged themselves in a circle, shooting multi-coloured spells in all directions. Glaurt, armed with a spiked club, swiped at the Badoch with abandon, sending shadowy figures flying.

But it wasn't the Badoch or the battle that made Avery's insides turn to ice. She shot a glance across at Ghilli and Low, and saw her own horror reflected in their faces. They had left Mab in the library, frozen under Acton's spell, so how was it possible that the dragon was battling against the witches right here at Canonmills?

27

The dragon prowled just out of reach of the witches' shooting spells, its tail flicking from side to side as it snapped and growled at the Badoch, urging them on. Even at this distance Avery could see that though the witches were furiously casting spells, they were massively outnumbered.

"How is that possible?" asked Avery in despair. "We've just left Mab! How can she be here?"

"I don't know, "said Wulver grimly. "But the dragon and the Badoch only need to wait for the witches to tire and then they'll be upon them."

Ghilli shook his head. "We need reinforcements."

"There's no time for that," replied Avery, scouring the scene below for some chink of hope. It wasn't supposed to be playing out like this. They had found Acton. Everything was supposed to be alright now. "We've got to go and help them!"

"Avery's right." Wulver leaned forward, whispering words of courage into Farl's ear. The horse plunged downwards, the others following close behind. They landed in the thick of the battle, the Badoch swarming on all sides. Spells fired left, right and centre. Immediately Wulver and Ghilli leapt down from their horses, pulling their bows from their backs and firing arrows into the ranks of the clamouring monsters.

"My lovelies!" Ceridwen's voice rang out over the noise. "What are you doing here?"

"Zis is no place for children!" cried Lilith, shooting a spell at a nearby Badoch.

The only member of the group who seemed pleased to see them was Glaurt, who beamed at Avery as he swung his club wildly. He almost looked like he was having fun.

"Behind you, Avery, honey!" shouted Jezebel.

Avery leapt just in time, a claw missing her by inches.

"I've got an idea!" cried Low, taking to the air. "Back in a minute."

Great, thought Avery to herself. What should she do? She didn't have a bow and arrow, and she couldn't fly... but she was fast!

Jumping and twisting, Avery used all of her Cat Fae skills to snake between the Badoch. She taunted them to follow, splitting eager Badoch from the safety of their ranks and making them easier for the others to pick off with a well-aimed spell or arrow. Up above, Low flew back and forth, dropping rocks and tree branches that he found around the park on the furious creatures.

Out of the corner of her eye Avery noticed the dragon suddenly raise its ugly head and sniff the air.

"I know you're here, Avery Buckle. I can *smell* you!" it hissed.

The dragon turned its head, scanning the battleground. When it spotted Avery, it crashed through the chaotic battle towards her.

Up close the dragon was terrifying. Its body was covered in massive scales, and enormous talons curled to sharp points at the end of powerful claws. It paused in front of her, flaming eyes meeting Avery's own.

"No, Avery!" Ghilli and Wulver shouted across the din. They tried to fight their way closer.

The dragon gave a nasty chuckle. "Well, well, Avery Buckle. I have you at last. I shall enjoy this!"

"You're not going to get away with this!" Avery spat out, her tail flicking angrily.

The dragon threw back its head and laughed. Then it lowered its face close. "You haven't worked out who I am yet have you, little kitty cat? Here's a clue: who's missing?"

Avery frowned back at the dragon. If it wasn't Mab, who else could it be? She looked around her. Ghilli, Wulver, Low and Glaurt were all there, and the witches. All except...

"Cassandra!" whispered Avery, stunned. "But... I don't understand."

"Of course you don't understand. You're a fool!" sneered Cassandra. "You think Mab is the only Logan? I'm her stepsister, born to Crux Logan's second wife. Though Mab would never recognise me as family. She only permitted my presence at Cunningfoot so she could keep a closer eye on me." She laughed again. "But alas, not close enough. I will complete my father's plans to wake the Crannog. I will rule everything and everyone!"

"And what about Acton?" Avery shouted, her disbelief turning to anger. "He was in your way, so you thought you would destroy him?"

"He betrayed me! I couldn't kill him because of you and your stupid heart bond," she spat. "You kept him alive with your nine lives, so I had to destroy him with the most powerful magic I could think of. I had to make sure he could never come back."

Never come back? Could it be that Cassandra still didn't know that Acton was alive? He had been right under her nose at the Lammermuirs' and she had no idea! Avery's frenzied thinking was interrupted by an enormous scaly claw that swept her off her feet.

"You, on the other hand," sneered Cassandra, squeezing Avery tight, "are much easier to kill. And I've hunted you for so long, Avery – I had no idea what you might look like each time you were reborn, so I had to get rid of every other mangy Cat Fae to find you!"

Avery felt suddenly sick. Cassandra was responsible for the Cat Fae disappearing?

Before Avery's thoughts could spiral further, there was a sudden whoosh of air, and a voice she knew very well commanded: "Madam, put her down!"

"Bob!" whooped Low, flying a loop-the-loop. "Bob and Cindy!"

It was Bob and Cindy, but not as Avery and Low had ever seen them before. Each of them shone brightly, their magic dazzling the dark throng of surrounding Badoch. Both of them carried gleaming swords and they looked furious.

Cassandra snarled and spat at them. "She's mine!"

"I hate to correct you, Madam," blazed Bob. "But she's actually ours!"

The talon around Avery tightened further. Cassandra lashed out at Bob and Cindy with her free claw, but they leapt nimbly backwards. Held up high, Avery had a good view of Cassandra's tail. She saw it tense, ready to strike.

"Look out!" she croaked.

Cindy raised her sword and brought down her blade on the dragon's flank. "You need to learn some manners, missy!"

There was a burst of light, then a long gash split open the dragon's scaly skin, red blood oozing from the wound. Avery found herself being flung into the air. She landed on the ground, the breath knocked out of her.

"Fools! You can't kill me!" the dragon roared.

Suddenly a rattling sound, accompanied by the frantic ringing of a bell, interrupted the dragon's cry and cut across the Badochs' menacing hisses and snarls. Two figures on a familiar-looking bicycle were racing down the bank, hurtling towards the deadly battle, the tandem's lamp blinking in warning.

Sparrow's handlebars swung wildly from side to side, the riders only just staying seated. As the bicycle whizzed towards Avery, she only had seconds to recognise Acton on the front seat, and a determined Mab perched on the back, her robes and red hair flying out behind her like flames.

28

Cassandra turned in an instant, planting her giant forelegs across Sparrow's path, barring the way.

"Get back!" she growled at the heaving Badoch, who pushed in on all sides, eager for prey. "Leave these two to me."

She watched the bicycle race towards her, one vicious claw poised mid-air. Avery jumped to her feet. Acton was desperately pulling on the brakes, but it was too late. With a lazy swipe Cassandra sent him, Mab and Sparrow flying into the air. Acton landed with a thud, crumpling to a heap on the ground.

"Acton!" screamed Avery. She ran to him, a horrible shooting pain piercing her chest. "Acton!"

Cassandra wheeled about in surprise, her eyes wide with shock.

"Acton?" She flicked the boy over carefully with one talon, her eyes scanning his face.

"That's right!" spat Avery as she sank to her knees beside him. She could hardly breathe. After all that had happened, Cassandra had torn him away from her again. Avery lifted her head and yelled through her tears, "Well, you finally did it. You killed him. You really are a monster!"

"Enough, Cassandra!" Mab rose and hobbled forward. "This has got to stop, sister! You have gone far enough. Turn back now from this terrible course, I beg of you. There is still hope."

Cassandra eyed her sister with rage.

"You! You are a traitor to the Logan name!"

Very slowly, and painfully, Mab raised her hands, as if in surrender.

Avery gasped. What was she doing?

"Wreak your punishment on me, Cassandra," Mab said quietly, "but let the others go. Let them go, and then leave this place. I will go with you... and I will submit to whatever punishment you see fit."

Mab looked like a queen, dignified and brave. Avery couldn't believe how wrong she had been about her. She was sacrificing herself for them all.

Cassandra tilted her huge dragon head, slowly considering, her hot breath shifting the flame-coloured hair around Mab's face. "Tempting," she murmured.

Then the snarling from the Badoch grew louder. They didn't want Mab. They wanted what Cassandra had promised them in exchange for their allegiance: total destruction. Cassandra seemed to hear them. She raised a massive claw and made a strange twisting movement.

As quick as lightning, a blue spark hit Mab squarely in the chest and she tumbled to the ground. The other witches cried out, but Cassandra gave a nasty snort.

"I am the one with the power!" she shrieked. "The... Crannog... is... m-mine..."

She faltered momentarily, clutching at her throat where the brass band circled her neck. She seemed to be having difficulty breathing.

"You... won't... s-stop me!" she gasped. She lurched to one side, confusion filling her eyes.

Avery got to her feet. Something odd was happening.

A high-pitched squeak rang out and then was suddenly cut short. All heads turned to Low, who sat on a branch in a nearby tree, mid-gulp. He flapped his wings awkwardly and hopped from foot to foot, as if embarrassed. A long pink tail hung down from his beak. With another gulp the tail was gone.

"Sorry!" he said, flapping his wings again. "I just saw it running around and suddenly came over all peckish. Have I... have I done something wrong?"

Cassandra slumped over with a mighty crash, her eyes glazed. "My rat!" she wheezed. She took one last heaving gasp. Her head rolled back and she lay finally still.

Ceridwen and Jezebel immediately ran to Mab,

cushioning her head and muttering healing spells, while Baba padded over to Low in her big slippers.

"I believe we owe you a debt of gratitude for saving us all, young Hoolet!" she said. "It seems you have unwittingly eaten Cassandra's rat. If I'm not very much mistaken, it would appear that she used heart-bond magic on the poor thing. While he lived, he was the only thing preventing that fatal wound of Cindy's from killing her. But now he's gone, she has too." Baba gazed down at the huge silent dragon sadly, gently closing its great eyes with a wrinkled hand.

She looked up at the snarling packs of Badoch. "Right then, ladies." Baba beckoned to the other witches, rubbing her hands together with a twinkle in her eye. "Time to dispense with this lot, I think!"

The witches raised their fingers and the black rolling mass of the Badoch scrambled to escape. A rainbow of sparks shot in all directions, illuminating the park.

Avery knelt beside Acton's body and gently stroked the hair away from his eyes. Low crouched beside her, back in his boy form.

"He can't be gone. Not after everything..." Avery whispered, biting her lip to stop more tears coming.

"Have you forgotten what Bean Nighe said?" asked Low kindly.

Avery blinked up at him, not understanding.

Low smiled. *"'He cannot die while you live'.* See?"

Avery looked down. Though it was very faint, the boy's chest moved up and down.

Acton Baxter was alive.

29

In the gardens below Edinburgh Castle, Avery and Baba watched as Ghilli skidded across the frozen surface of the fountain's pool, calling out to Acton and Low to race him. Wulver stood at a distance chuckling, never a fan of water, even less so when it was icy cold. The temperature had plummeted since the battle at Canonmills two weeks ago, and icicles hung like glistening jewels from the statues that decorated the pretty turquoise and gold fountain. Winter was on its way.

Avery was warm and snug in her thick cloak. She could hear festive songs and the chatter of people from the Christmas market nearby. Lights sparkled and the enticing aromas of hot chocolate and roasted chestnuts mingled in the air.

"So the Crannog remains asleep in its watery cavern below the city, all thanks to you," said Baba, tracing a woody knot on the bench they sat on.

"No," replied Avery. "All thanks to Low. He was the one who ate Cassandra's rat! And it was predicted in the prophecy, if we'd only known." She recited the familiar words:

"Tale bites tale, pierced heart,
family bonds and corrupted arts,
Flame-red hair, kindles bad,
rodent-hearted and power-mad,
Memories lost, dark loch,
hidden path 'neath city rock,
Magic man, youth reborn,
preserved awhile by Cat Fae lore,
Hearts bond, hearts weep,
hearts told and histories keep,
Forgotten beast, foot to claw,
airborne, the Great Wyrm's flaw,
Tales stolen, tales remade,
by a tale told, a history's paid."

Avery smiled. "Cassandra was the rodent-hearted one with flame-red hair, and Low was the airborne forgotten beast who was the dragon's – or the Great Wyrm's – downfall."

Baba nodded thoughtfully. "I told you prophecies never make sense until they do. They're tricky like that. Did you hear that Tutt Pugh's tail has grown back?"

"No? That's amazing!"

"It's more than that, it's unheard of. Yes, lots of things are returning. Gradually our memories are coming back to us, only in fragments of course. You reminded us, you see, just as Acton asked you to in your vision. And Odin sang you into legend, which helped too. And now with Acton found, the return of a Cat Fae to Scotland, and Hoolets back from extinction, we're all hopeful that the balance of the magical world may be restored in time."

Avery nodded, thinking back to her conversation with Acton in her vision. "Baba, when I saw the old Acton at the Lammermuirs' gatehouse, he wondered where our memory casket had gone."

"Indeed. Did he?" asked Baba.

"We must have one, just like Whimbrel and his Cat Fae. I was thinking that if I could find it I might be able to find out about my parents. Do..." Avery hesitated. "Do you know where it might be, Baba?"

Baba regarded her sorrowfully. "No, Avery, I'm sorry. Slowly but surely things are coming back to me, but I do think some things may be lost forever. And of course, there are things that I never knew in the first place."

While Avery was sad that she might never know the truth about her past, or the extent of Cassandra's crimes against the Cat Fae, she also felt peaceful. She found herself repeating the words she had spoken to Wulver on the way to Orkney. "I think there are lots of ways of belonging. When nobody else would believe me about Acton, it was my friends who stuck by me and helped me find the truth.

Low, Ghilli and Wulver, even the Stones, they were the ones who believed me. Even if I never find out who my parents were, I think I've found where I belong."

Baba patted Avery's arm. "Yes, belonging is a powerful thing. Your bond with Acton is proof of that. When you were reborn, so was he. Knuckle found him at the Lammermuirs' as a baby and kept him safe all those years."

"Were you the witch who told Knuckle to hide him?" asked Avery curiously.

"Yes," said Baba. "Though I only have a vague memory of it." She frowned. "I must have known then that you were both in danger – and that your survival would be vital for us all in the years to come."

Avery loosened her tail from where it had coiled around her leg and admired its black silkiness. She didn't hide it any more. She knew now that it was as much a part of her as Acton was. Her eyes followed him as he skidded, giggling, across the ice after Ghilli. With a twitch of his finger Acton thawed one of the fountain jets, sending a burst of water across the faery's path, causing him to spin off and tumble over the pool's edge. Acton's magic was slowly starting to emerge, though he was partial to using it for mischief.

Avery couldn't imagine life without him now.

A tall figure stood on the other side of the fountain,

a safe distance away from the action. A thin smile spread across Mab's haughty face as she watched the boys' antics.

"I need to apologise to Mab," said Avery. "I was taken in by Cassandra because she was kind, while Mab was forbidding. I accused her of such terrible things." Avery shook her head. "I jumped to so many conclusions – Mab and Cassandra have the same red hair, but I was determined that it was Mab in the railway tunnel. And I thought she smashed the memory casket in the library and killed the book, but it was Cassandra all along. The vision I saw was Mab hiding it after Whimbrel's death to keep it safe. Then after all that, we shut her in a cupboard and froze her!" Avery felt her face flush with shame. They had been lucky that Acton had struggled to recast his spell at the library, giving Mab and Edgar the chance to convince him that she wasn't to blame.

"Mab can be rather stern," said Baba. "But I think she'd appreciate your apology, Avery. She has always had to prove herself to those who would judge her by her Logan name alone. And though Cassandra lost her way, she was still Mab's sister – a kind word or two wouldn't go astray."

It was Low's turn to race Acton around the fountain, but he was ready for the water-jet trick, swooping up into the air and deflecting the spray of freezing water over

Acton with his wing tip. Ghilli hooted with glee as Acton grinned up from under his dripping fringe.

"What happens now, Baba? Where do we go?" asked Avery uncertainly.

"Ah, yes, we've been discussing that. Bob and Cindy are quite taken by the idea of going to live with Knuckle."

"But—"

"You don't need them any more, Avery," Baba explained kindly. "They looked after you while you had to be hidden, and protected you from Cassandra at Canonmills, but you're safe now. I suppose you've guessed by now that Bob never did really collect cheese graters?"

Avery shook her head, amused at how she had been fooled. "He was polishing those swords, wasn't he?"

"Indeed. Keeping them ready, just in case you needed protection. All part of their guardian magic. They came in very handy as it turned out. And now, well, Bob is keen to try out his DIY skills on the Lammermuirs' castle, and I believe Cindy has been buying interior-design magazines. Of course, as guardians, they will always be there for you should you need them, but for the moment they can keep the castle safe until the family returns. Although I don't think it will ever be quite right until they do.

"You'll have to go and see for yourself sometime.

I think Knuckle likes the idea of it being a second home for you and Acton. Not that he would ever admit it."

Avery laughed. She could well imagine.

"But for now, well, it's nearly Christmas and I think we could all do with a holiday," said Baba. "There's nowhere like Inchmahome at Christmas. You should see how they light up the island. It's magic. Quite literally!"

"I'd love to go, and I'm sure Acton would." Avery beamed, her eyes shining. "Low too!"

"And after that…" continued Baba, swinging her short legs to and fro off the bench.

"Yes, after that?" asked Avery.

Baba nodded towards Acton with a wry smile. "That boy is going to need some tuition if he's going to become the great wizard we all know he is, and you a powerful Cat Fae. We are all agreed that if you would be willing, we'd like you and Acton to come to Cunningfoot and live with us. You'll be able to visit Low whenever you wish – we'll set up a doorway. Lillith has agreed to help him find out more about his Hoolet history, so we'll be seeing lots of him, I'm sure."

Avery squealed with delight, wrapping her arms around Baba and kissing her crinkly cheeks. "That would be amazing, Baba!"

"Dear, dear," the old witch chuckled, fondly smoothing out a tangle in Avery's hair.

"Acton! Acton!" Avery called across the park, unable to hold her excitement in.

He looked up from where he was conjuring a ball of snow in his palm from a handful of icy water, half an eye on the back of Wulver's head.

"Baba says we can live with her and the witches at Cunningfoot!" she shouted. "And we're going to Inchmahome for Christmas! You too, Low!"

"YES!" whooped Low, swooping down. "If the food at the Autumn Feast is anything to go by, imagine what Christmas dinner will be like!"

Acton beamed over at Avery, launching his snowball at her instead. "A home together at Cunningfoot? Let's grow a peach tree!"

Avery managed to catch the snowball without it collapsing in her hand. This whole adventure had started with a peach stone dragging her across the night sky, so growing a peach tree in their new home seemed like the perfect ending, or perhaps it was a kind of beginning…

"Alright then," she laughed, and threw the snowball back at him. Avery was so happy she felt she might burst. She had a home. She belonged. And all because she had followed her heart.

ACKNOWLEDGEMENTS

Firstly to Floris Books for the wonder that is the Kelpies Prize. Thank you for being willing to grow writers, nurturing them with encouragement and opportunity.

The Kelpies team who are a wonderful, friendly, talented bunch of people. I am so lucky to have your expertise behind this book. Particular thanks to Jennie and Eleanor, whose creativity, patience, positivity and willingness to go the extra mile have made this book what it is. I have learnt so much from you and will be forever grateful.

Xavier Bonet for the perfect cover artwork. Check out Xavier's work at www.xavierbonet.net

The Turner/Evans clan, who gave me my love of books, thought it entirely normal to give a ten year old *The Complete Works of Arthur Conan Doyle* for Christmas, and who only listen with half an ear to my book-related pursuits. I love you.

The mighty tribe of Foleys, Goodens, Taits, Tyas', Bedsons and Pearces. Thank you for your Glaurt-the-troll-sized love and support. So glad to be on your team.

Frances and Linda for hats.

Linda (again!) and Gemma for enthusiastic support.

Lindsey, for catch-ups and wise words.

SCBWI friends, who share expertise and cheer each other on so generously.

My patients, graciously battling impossible situations. For perspective.

Tess and my littlies, who remind me daily of the importance of joyful wonder.

Rich, my best friend in the whole wide world.

And finally, you the reader. Thank you for coming on this adventure with me and Avery. May you always be brave enough for a second look under the sofa cushion or a hard stare at that crack in the pavement. Magical adventures await!

You might also enjoy...

'The Nowhere Emporium is up there with Ollivanders as a magical place that readers will want to explore again and again.' – *The Guardian*

Winner of a Blue Peter Best Story Award and a Scottish Children's Book Award.

When the mysterious Nowhere Emporium arrives in Glasgow, orphan Daniel Holmes stumbles upon it quite by accident. Before long, the 'shop from nowhere' – and its owner, Mr Silver – draw Daniel into a breathtaking world of magic and enchantment.

 Also available as an eBook

DiscoverKelpies.co.uk

'From the first word, readers are dropped straight into the lively action, with nary a breather until the final page turn.' – *Kirkus Reviews*

Curses aren't real. Magic is only in stories. So Molly Drummond definitely can't be magically cursed. Can she?

When Molly attends a curse-lifting workshop run by a local witch, she tumbles into a world of magical beings, dark danger and extraordinary friendship in the first book of Lari Don's breathtaking *Spellchasers* trilogy.

 Also available as an eBook

DiscoverKelpies.co.uk

"Fantastically enchanting."

GUARDIANS OF THE WILD UNICORNS

LINDSAY LITTLESON

I know it's a crazy plan, and you don't need to come with me. But I'm going to find the unicorns, and when I find them, I'm going to set them free.

In the wild Scottish highlands, best friends Lewis and Rhona discover that the legends are true: unicorns are real creatures, darkly magical and in deadly danger.

Can the friends rescue the wild unicorns before an ancient promise has unimagined consequences for them all?

 Also available as an eBook

DiscoverKelpies.co.uk

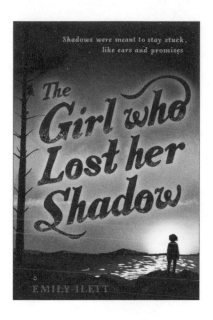

Shadows were meant to stay stuck, like ears and promises.

On the morning of Gail's birthday, her shadow escapes.
She's not surprised it decided to leave. Her dad has gone
for good. Her big sister Kay, once Gail's best friend,
has disappeared into sadness — and now her shadow has
left too.

Determined to make things right, Gail's search for
the shadows takes her to unexpected places and she
soon discovers that she's not the only one looking for
something missing...

 Also available as an eBook

DiscoverKelpies.co.uk